MW00834777

The Fairy Tales of Hans Christian ANDERSEN

Edited by
Noel Daniel

Art Direction by
Andy Disl *and* Noel Daniel

TASCHEN

Introduction
by Noel Daniel
6

*Credits &
Acknowledgments*
188

Hans Christian Andersen

The Heart and Soul of the Modern Fairy Tale

by Noel Daniel

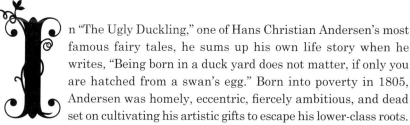

n "The Ugly Duckling," one of Hans Christian Andersen's most famous fairy tales, he sums up his own life story when he writes, "Being born in a duck yard does not matter, if only you are hatched from a swan's egg." Born into poverty in 1805, Andersen was homely, eccentric, fiercely ambitious, and dead set on cultivating his artistic gifts to escape his lower-class roots. In his lifetime, he would win praise as one of Denmark's most important writers. By the end of his life, he was regularly feted and kept the company of kings. Today, he is known as the most famous Scandinavian writer ever. But his rags-to-riches story was not without childhood misjudgment and maltreatment by others, deep anguish, and heartbreak, which was the engine of his ambitions. While these experiences created a relentless need for recognition, Andersen's brilliant talent for storytelling and his gift for everyday language spawned a whole new kind of fairy tale and have endeared him to millions since his first collection was published in 1835.

The Spinning Room
as Laboratory for Listening

The old women in the lunatic asylum in Andersen's hometown of Odense spun tales to amuse themselves as they spun their yarn. While Andersen's paternal grandmother tended the garden, a young Hans Christian gravitated

to the spinning room—the social heart of the asylum and a traditional hub of tale telling. It was a room full of chatter, gossip, sweat, and cackles, alive with the rhythmic motion of the spinners, and the click and clack of their wheels. It was a laboratory for listening. There, Andersen heard all manner of peasant folk tales in the oral tradition. Typical of Scandinavian folklore, they were full of supernatural creatures such as goblins, trolls, witches, and water spirits. "A world as rich as that of *The Thousand and One Nights* was revealed to me," wrote Andersen later in one of his autobiographies. "The stories told by these old ladies, and the insane figures which I saw around me in the asylum, operated in the meantime so powerfully upon me, that when it grew dark I scarcely dared go out of the house."

This spontaneous, messy, vibrant, living oral tradition was the Holy Grail to a growing number of scholars and Romantic writers in Europe. Learned academics like the Brothers Grimm in Germany sought to preserve this very same colloquial and unrefined art form in their collection of German fairy tales, which was first published in 1812, when Andersen was seven years old. Andersen would read the tales later as a young writer, and much later he visited the Grimms as an established one.

PAGE 2 AND FAR LEFT *The "Thumbelina" image on page 2 by British artist Eleanor Vere Boyle is from her 1872 book, far left, one of the first color books of Andersen's tales. Illustrated children's books like this were non-existent in Andersen's youth.*

PAGE 4 *"The Nightingale," from 1843, about a songbird supplanted by an artificial one, is considered one of Andersen's masterpieces, and Kay Nielsen's 1924 illustration captures its otherworldly fantasy. When younger,*

Andersen had been called "the Nightingale of Funen" for his voice. He also fell in love with singer Jenny Lind, "the Swedish Nightingale," but his feelings were unreciprocated.

LEFT *By the 1920s, the children's book industry in Europe was in its golden age, and the influential Danish artist Kay Nielsen was one of its luminaries. His 1924 book of Andersen tales, near left, included the tender, striking image of a frozen heart from "The Snow Queen," page 6.*

From Superstitious World to Imagination on Fire

Contrary to popular perception, the Grimms did not travel the countryside gathering oral stories, but relied heavily on a few trusted sources, both oral and literary. By contrast, Andersen's exposure was the real deal: He grew up in the thick of a superstitious society where oral tales were a source of entertainment as well as purveyors of life lessons. In Andersen's youth, Odense was Denmark's second-largest city, with 8,000 inhabitants, and was still more a medieval town with traditional customs than an urban hub like Copenhagen.

These centuries-old Scandinavian stories were part of an oral culture that colored Andersen's childhood, and the peasant tales he heard would eventually all but vanish as the countryside was industrialized and the social habits of the lower classes changed. Fairy-tale historians Iona and Peter Opie note that "Andersen was in fact the first writer of fairy tales to come—as the Grimms with their professional background did not—from the humble class to whom storytelling was a living tradition. All the people who surrounded him in his childhood, other than his father, were people who relied on word of mouth, not on books, for their knowledge." His mother, who by all accounts loved her son very much, visited fortune-tellers and, deeply superstitious, explained all manner of phenomena by ghosts and goblins. For those in Andersen's immediate

This 1929 book of Andersen's longest tale,
"The Snow Queen," features beautiful Art Deco
endpapers and images by Katharine Beverley
and Elizabeth Ellender (see pages 102–149).
It is a spectacular example of two-tone printing
used to produce beauty on a budget, which
exemplified the Art Deco idea of creating high-
quality decorative art for everyday life.

orbit inclined toward superstition, inanimate objects literally had minds of their own. Andersen's masterful ability to anthropomorphize objects became a hallmark of his work.

Unable to read or write, Andersen's mother was a washerwoman and later succumbed to alcoholism. Andersen's father was a shoemaker by trade who loved literature and, remarkably for the time, owned a cupboard of books. Until he died when Andersen was eleven, he read stories and plays to his son regularly, among them *The Thousand and One Nights* and the Bible. Thanks to his father, who had carved out his own rudimentary education against all odds, Andersen's early and loving introduction to the printed page led to a lifetime of voracious reading. Andersen wrote in his diary, "From as early as I can remember, reading was my sole and my most loved pastime ... I never played with other boys, I was always alone."

Reading suited Andersen's temperament and powers of imagination to a T. But Andersen was also a great listener—in the spinning room of the asylum, to his father's story time, to the actors of the theater he adored. He listened acutely to the characters and voices around him, and it trained his ear. He developed an inner ear for the sights and sounds of whole imaginary worlds, like the haughty tone of the deluded sewing needle in "The Darning Needle," or the emperor's comical inner monologue of self-doubt in "The Emperor's New Clothes," or the little silver bells in the palace

flowers that "tinkled so that no one could pass by without noticing them" in "The Nightingale." No person or thing in the real world escaped Andersen's notice as a potential character.

"I Will Become Famous"

"I will become famous," Andersen wrote in his diary, underscoring that his professional drive to greatness was not the polite narcissism of the restrained and well educated. His drive to greatness ran deep in the troubled psychic waters of his soul. Early on, his patrons recognized a powerful self-confidence in Andersen. He possessed a gritty drive to perform, a marvelous soprano voice (before it cracked), a gift for telling stories, and, along with all of this, an irritating ego.

Andersen sought recognition all of his life. Historians tell us that his letters reveal he was privately haunted by feelings of inadequacy and loneliness. Andersen never married, and experienced several instances of unrequited love that scarred him deeply. For a romantic with a profound sense of pathos and for a lifelong bachelor who enjoyed the warm, secure family lives of his close friends, he was haunted by a life devoid of reciprocated love. One such instance was to the famous Swedish singer Jenny Lind, "the Swedish Nightingale" who served as the inspiration for Andersen's tale "The Nightingale." He himself had been called "the

Another mistaken-identity story is his well-known tale "The Princess and the Pea," famously illustrated here by Kay Nielsen in 1925.

Nightingale of Funen" as a boy, referring to the island on which Odense lies. Born into poverty and rising to fame through their artistic talent, Lind and Andersen had much in common. But his infatuation with her was not reciprocated.

Ascending the Social Ranks through Poetry

While it was oral storytelling that helped shape Andersen's mind and his literary voice, it was the democratization of Danish society that opened up doors for him that in the past would have been closed to someone with Andersen's background. Part of Andersen's genius lay in his ability to somehow perceive, while growing up in the poorest corner of Odense, that high society was mobile enough that if he cracked it, he would go far. He armored himself with steely ambition, an electric imagination, and not an ounce of stage fright as he tried first to break into the ranks of theater in Copenhagen. But he also cultivated what was necessary to move ahead: "Andersen was quick to realize that socially, poetry was a winning card," biographer Jackie Wullschlager observes. She goes on, "this was a time when art and literature stood at the intellectual core of the nation, because political life was barely allowed to exist." In the face of the absolute monarchy that ruled Denmark until 1848, "artistic life ... consumed the

energy that other nations were pouring into politics, and the result was a Golden Age of culture, a flowering of painting, music, literature and philosophy, unprecedented in Danish history."

Royal patronage dependent on good breeding and connections was way out of Andersen's league, and his path to success was fraught with deprivation and repeated rejection. But incredibly, he persisted. Ultimately, he was noticed by the director of the Royal Theater, Jonas Collin, who helped secure a royal stipend for the teenager. What followed was a painful five-year period of being schooled with eleven-year-olds when Andersen was seventeen at the insistence of his sponsors. They had demanded that he either get a proper education before advancing as a writer, or go home and learn a trade. The latter had been the fate of his father and was absolutely out of the question for Andersen. But sprinkled in these experiences was just enough positive reinforcement, and with Collin's vital help, Andersen would go on to receive an artist's allowance that gave him the time and energy to write. Collin and his son would remain important figures throughout Andersen's life, and the closest thing to family he would know as an adult.

This cover detail, as well as the illustrations on pages 152–169, by famous Dutch illustrator Theo van Hoytema, are from his 1893 book Het Leelijke Jonge Eendje (The Ugly Duckling) *and show his love of Art Nouveau. One of Andersen's most famous lines comes from this story of mistaken identity and discrimination, often interpreted as autobiographical: "Being born in a duck yard does not matter, if only you are hatched from a swan's egg."*

A Poor Peasant in a Royal Mantle

Andersen was forever dancing between self-assuredness and feelings of inferiority and emotional vulnerability. He never escaped feeling unequal to the royals, celebrities, and dignitaries he socialized with as his fame grew, writing in his diary, "I had and still have a feeling as though I were a poor peasant lad over whom a royal mantle is thrown." But he seems to have also drawn considerable strength from his rags-to-riches story, which he eulogized frequently to others. He valued the hardship and tribulation that shaped his life. The genre of fairy tales must have instinctively felt comfortable for their prevalence of centuries-old rags-to-riches fantasies and tales of mistaken identity, where a dimwit is shown through trial and tribulation to be a true royal, if not by blood then by character. Andersen immortalized this theme in many tales, from "The Ugly Duckling" to "The Princess and the Pea" and "Thumbelina."

Andersen continued to be artistically inspired by his childhood for his whole life. Modern-day behavioral psychologists would call Andersen's childhood steeped in imaginative play (albeit alone), play-acting, and role-taking that strengthens the child's imagination and executive function. Andersen did this every day, forgoing the company of boys his own age for his puppet theater and doll costumes, seeing creative projects from inception to completion, adapting different voices to different characters, cultivating his own interests and instincts for storytelling.

Sweeter than
Chocolate and Cream

Andersen wrote his fairy tales for both adults and children. But his inner ear was writing for what historians have called "the listening child." It was his own childlike ability to remain open to the sights and sounds of the world that allowed him to write so effectively for children. This was a radical development in children's literature, which had previously been made up primarily of morality tales.

In a 1928 illustrated book of Andersen's stories by the Japanese artist Takeo Takei, the Japanese publisher describes Andersen's tales as "sweeter than chocolate and cream." Contemporary readers might find it hard to imagine just how different Andersen's tales were from those before them. They were beautifully paced and passionate, at times sorrowful and full of pathos, and at other times wickedly funny. Simply put, they were a pleasure to read, and they spoke directly to children's sensibilities rather than condescending to them. As the Japanese publisher aptly sensed, Andersen's tales arrived on the scene like dessert after centuries of hard-to-swallow didacticism and flavorless moral teachings in children's literature (although Andersen was careful to sprinkle in moral lessons and Christian adages befitting his middle-class audience).

This cover of Japanese legend Takeo Takei's 1928 book of Andersen's tales shows a tin soldier, whose love for a paper ballerina is immortalized in "The Steadfast Tin Soldier." Andersen's ability to give objects voices became a unique characteristic of his stories. Takei's Japanese publisher called Andersen's tales "sweeter than chocolate and cream." They spoke directly to children's sensibilities and were like dessert after centuries of hard-to-swallow didacticism and flavorless moral teachings in children's literature. From them sprang the modern legacy of stories told from the child's perspective in a world of make-believe.

Children's Stories for Children's Sake

Andersen had tasted an art form that didn't yet exist beyond his own tales: children's stories for children's sake. Wullschlager calls Andersen the world's first great fantasy storyteller: "He used speaking toys and animals, and he gave them voices, easy, colloquial and funny, with which children could instantly identify." From Andersen's tales springs the modern legacy of stories told from the child's perspective in a world of make-believe, from *Alice in Wonderland* to *The Wizard of Oz* to *Toy Story*. This "new" perspective is the core of two of the most modern genres: animation and cartoon.

Where the Brothers Grimm, both trained academics and linguists, were inspired by the direct language and powerful emotional imagery that flavored folk tales, Andersen wore his heart on his sleeve. Describing himself as apolitical, Andersen writes in one of his autobiographies, "God has imparted to me another mission: that I felt, and that I feel still." He was a romantic by constitution, not by choice, and it made life hard for him. As he matured as a writer, he discovered that the poetry and emotional vulnerabilities of the German Romantics flowering in Europe were very literally balm for his introspective and brooding soul.

Although Andersen's tales were as poetic and emotionally disclosing as the literature of the German Romantics, they were also highly modern

Vincent van Gogh, a contemporary of Andersen, was so stunned by the visual details of Andersen's tales that he claimed he must have been a visual artist too. In fact, Andersen was an avid paper cutter. He learned the skill as a child, and often produced paper cuttings at social gatherings. At right are two examples of the hundreds he made: a circular pattern from 1844 of swans and dancing Pierrots, a favorite motif, and a Pierrot with a tree and dancer from ca. 1866.

in that their subjects and style were rooted in everyday contemporary life, not in a glorified or idealized past, which was a hallmark of older "Once upon a time" fairy tales, with their caste systems. His break with what Andersen biographer Reginald Spink calls "academic conventions" resembled the rifts created on the brink of modernity by avant-garde European artists tired of the soulless restrictions of academic artistic practices. The painter van Gogh, a contemporary of Andersen, was so stunned by the visual details of Andersen's fairy tales that he claimed he must have been a visual artist too (in fact, he was an avid and skilled paper cutter, often producing paper cuttings at social gatherings). Andersen's style was dreamy yet sensual, and the worlds depicted in his tales existed in a completely formed emotional ecosystem of its own logic.

In Search of Immortality

Even though Andersen grew up surrounded by Danish folk tales, he made up his own, rather than collecting them like the Brothers Grimm had. In 1835 Andersen released a small booklet of his first four tales. According to Danish folk tale expert Bengt Holbek, only seven of Andersen's over 200 tales are based on pre-existing ones. When a close friend told him that if his first successful novel, *The Improvisatore* (1835), had made him

famous, these tales would make him immortal, "for they are the most perfect things [you] have written," Andersen reflected, "I myself do not think so." Andersen had found his form, although he did not yet know it. In fact, the psychology that pervaded Andersen's tales was new and fresh, and his tales literally touched a nerve in pre-modern Europe. While his introspection and sensitivity were imperfectly calibrated to the demands of his own life, Andersen had the ability to articulate desires petty and profound and make them into transcendent tales. Andersen's fairy tales have had so great an influence on children's literature since that the two most important awards in children's literature for writing and illustration are called the Hans Christian Andersen Awards, and his birthday, April 2, was chosen as International Children's Book Day.

Between his mother's superstitions, his father's prolific reading and fawning over the young Andersen with homemade puppet theaters and toys, the pictures and green branches gathered by his mother that covered their home, and Andersen's own love of reading, there was a lot of mental and visual activity taking place in their one-room cottage during his childhood. It is no wonder that he was a daydreamer, often escaping into his own private thoughts. The safe, internal world of his imagination would become the infinite well of his creative writing. His mind was primed to leap at inspiration instantly. Wullschlager quotes Andersen describing the way his mind worked: "[Ideas] lay in

Tom Seidmann-Freud, niece of Sigmund Freud,
was a groundbreaking children's bookmaker.
Her 1921 book Kleine Märchen (Little Fairy Tales)
includes an early version of her artwork for
"The Princess and the Pea," on this book's cover
and pages 28/29.

my thoughts like a seed corn, requiring only a flowing stream, a ray of sunshine, a drop from the cup of bitterness, for them to spring forth and burst into bloom."

A Glimpse of the Unconscious
in Early Modernity

Historians have speculated that Andersen's fairy tales are in fact early tales of the unconscious that presaged artistic movements of the early twentieth century and later Surrealism. While artists and thinkers such as Freud in the modern era tried to capture the unconscious or, in the case of many modern artists, unleash its creative potential, Andersen's approach was to stand ready to act on the wild inspiration within his own mind.

The tumult of his childhood and the persistent bumpy road he experienced as a social outsider could have easily embittered him for a lifetime and dispirited him to the point of giving up his dreams. But Andersen's drive—also described by historians as a belief in his own special destiny—made him eternally prepared. While the critical reception of Andersen's plays, travel writings, and novels has shown them to be somewhat uneven artistically, his fairy tales remain brilliant examples of his unique imagination and his obvious total comfort in and mastery of the imaginary

worlds he conjured in his mind, a safe place to which he returned time and time again in the face of adversity. It was there that he integrated his emotions with reality. Fairy-tale historian Jack Zipes writes: "His fairy tales were of the life he did not lead, and they spoke what he wanted to say publicly but did not dare. His writings were majestic acts of self-affirmation and self-deception."

The Pain and Pleasure of Subjectivity

Andersen imbues a simple inkstand, a toy soldier, a bird, a pea, a spinning top with their own drives, blind spots, desires, arrogances, and courage. Andersen's characters are humanlike in their passions as well as their frailties, and often have a slightly kinked perspective, unable to see their real fate or position, as if Andersen were shining a light on the limitations of our own human subjectivity. In this way, perhaps the real subject of his tales is the inescapable condition of subjectivity as the essence of human experience.

But it is precisely this subjectivity that also allows for love, to be deeply possessed by one's own experience, to become engulfed and even consumed by caring for another person. For Andersen, this is both a powerful creative engine and a source for potential hurt and disappointment. His

"The Little Mermaid" by British artist Jennie Harbour, from Hans Andersen's Stories, *1932.*

tales are infused with the enormous depth of feeling he was capable of, but which remained unfulfilled in his own life. Zipes writes of Andersen's relationship to his own personal story: "Andersen tried desperately to give his life the form and content of a fairy tale, precisely because he was a troubled, lonely, and highly neurotic artist who sublimated in literary creation his failure to fulfill his wishes and dreams in reality. His literary fame rests on this failure, for what he was unable to achieve for himself he created for millions of readers, young and old, with the hope that their lives might be different from his." The imperfect, unresolved psychological recesses and emotional landscapes in children's tales were his gifts to us, and his heart and soul took refuge there.

THE TALES

The Princess
and the Pea

Although this tale is one of Andersen's shortest, it is also one of his most famous—satirical, comical, and irreverent, all in just a few hundred words. It tells
of a stranded princess who arrives at the castle of a prince who has been searching for a true princess to marry. A pea is tucked into her bed to test her sensitivity, and thus her royalty. The humorous image of a sleepless night caused by a
pea has made its way into our everyday lexicon as a metaphor for acute delicacy.
Some historians have interpreted the tale as Andersen mocking—or praising—
his own sensitivity; others have speculated he was poking fun at thin-skinned
royalty. This 1835 tale was one of his first. While most of his tales are original, he
adapted this one from oral folk tales he heard as a child, and as he wrote of
these early tales to a friend, "I have written them completely as I would tell them
to a *child*." The tales, however, received harsh reviews at first, with some aghast at
their colloquial language—a brazen act at the time and an approach that eventually won Andersen fame as an innovator.—ND

Watercolor-and-ink illustration by Tom Seidmann-Freud, German, 1921

nce there was a prince who wanted to marry a princess. Only a real one would do. So he traveled through all the world to find her, and everywhere things went wrong. There were princesses aplenty, but how was he to know whether they were real princesses? There was something not quite right about them all. So he came home again and was unhappy, because he did so want to have a real princess.

One evening a terrible storm blew up. It lightninged and thundered and rained. It was really frightful! In the midst of it all came a knocking at the town gate. The old king went to open it.

Who should be standing outside but a princess, and what a sight she was in all that rain and wind. Water streamed from her hair down her clothes into her shoes, and ran out at the heels. Yet she claimed to be a real princess.

"We'll soon find that out," the old queen thought to herself. Without saying a word about it she went to the bedchamber, stripped back the bedclothes, and put just one pea in the bottom of the bed. Then she took twenty mattresses and piled them on

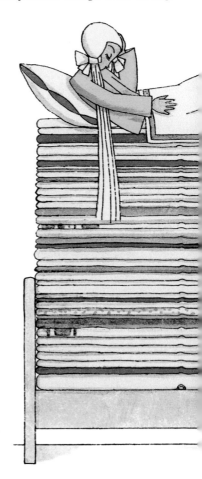

In the morning they asked her, "Did you sleep well?"
"Oh!" said the princess. "No. I scarcely slept at all.
Heaven knows what's in that bed."

the pea. Then she took twenty eiderdown feather beds and piled them on the mattresses. Up on top of all these the princess was to spend the night.

In the morning they asked her, "Did you sleep well?"

"Oh!" said the princess. "No. I scarcely slept at all. Heaven knows what's in that bed. I lay on something so hard that I'm black and blue all over. It was simply terrible."

They could see she was a real princess and no question about it, now that she had felt one pea all the way through twenty mattresses and twenty more feather beds. Nobody but a princess could be so delicate. So the prince made haste to marry her, because he knew he had found a real princess.

As for the pea, they put it in a museum. There it's still to be seen, unless somebody has taken it.

There, that's a true story.

The Nightingale

When Andersen published his famous story "The Nightingale" in 1843, about a songbird cast aside for a beautiful artificial one, it helped cement his reputation as a brilliant writer. Critics hailed the story as a poetic masterpiece. Since Andersen wrote most of his tales from scratch, he often wove in inspiration from real life. Historians cite as an example his love for the singing sensation Jenny Lind, nicknamed "the Swedish Nightingale." Although his love was not reciprocated, he felt a profound artistic kinship to her: He was called "the Nightingale of Funen" in his early years as an aspiring singer, and like Lind, with her soulful singing, so different from the era's complex operatic style, Andersen chose a relatively natural style of writing. The tale's Chinese theme was inspired by the chinoiserie of Copenhagen's new Tivoli Gardens. But arguably the tale's most important legacy is the heartfelt insight it gives into Andersen's thoughts about art and the challenges of following one's convictions, even if it means being alone in one's artistic vision. At a time of gradual democratization in Europe, he was experiencing first-hand the diversification of what constituted genius.—ND

Silhouettes with colored details by Georgiĭ Ivanovich Narbut, Ukrainian, 1912

To the prettiest flowers were tied little silver bells
that tinkled so that no one could pass by without noticing them.

The emperor of China is a Chinaman, as you most likely know, and everyone around him is a Chinaman, too. It's been a great many years since this story happened in China, but that's all the more reason for telling it before it gets forgotten.

The emperor's palace was the wonder of the world. It was made entirely of fine porcelain, extremely expensive but so delicate that you could touch it only with the greatest of care. In the garden the rarest flowers bloomed, and to the prettiest ones were tied little silver bells that tinkled so that no one could pass by without noticing them. Yes, all things were arranged according to plan in the emperor's garden, though how far and wide it extended not even the gardener knew. If you walked on and on, you came to a fine forest where the trees were tall and the lakes were deep. The forest ran down to the deep blue sea, so close that tall ships could sail under the branches of the trees. In these trees a nightingale lived. His song was so ravishing that even the poor fisherman, who had much else to do, stopped to listen on the nights when he went out to cast his nets, and heard the nightingale.

"How beautiful that is," he said, but he had his work to attend to, and he would forget the bird's song. But the next night, when he heard the song he would again say, "How beautiful."

From all the countries in the world travelers came to the city of the emperor. They admired the city. They admired the palace and its garden, but when they heard the nightingale they said, "That is the best of all."

And the travelers told of it when they came home, and men of learning wrote many books about the town, about the palace, and about the garden. But they did not forget the nightingale. They praised him highest of all, and those who were poets wrote magnificent poems about the nightingale who lived in the forest by the deep sea.

Then the nightingale sang. "That's it," said the little kitchen girl.
"Listen, listen! And yonder he sits." "Is it possible?"
cried the lord-in-waiting.

These books went all the world over, and some of them came even to the emperor of China. He sat in his golden chair and read, and read, nodding his head in delight over such glowing descriptions of his city, and palace, and garden. *But the nightingale is the best of all.* He read it in print.

"What's this?" the emperor exclaimed. "I don't know of any nightingale. Can there be such a bird in my empire—in my own garden—and I not know it? To think that I should have to learn of it out of a book."

Thereupon he called his lord-in-waiting, who was so exalted that when anyone of lower rank dared speak to him, or ask him a question, he only answered, "P," which means nothing at all.

"They say there's a most remarkable bird called the nightingale," said the emperor. "They say it's the best thing in all my empire. Why haven't I been told about it?"

"I've never heard the name mentioned," said the lord-in-waiting. "He hasn't been presented at court."

"I command that he appear before me this evening, and sing," said the emperor. "The whole world knows my possessions better than I do!"

"I never heard of him before," said the lord-in-waiting. "But I shall look for him. I'll find him."

But where? The lord-in-waiting ran upstairs and downstairs, through all the rooms and corridors, but no one he met with had ever heard tell of the nightingale. So the lord-in-waiting ran back to the emperor, and said it must be a story invented by those who write books. "Your Imperial Majesty would scarcely believe how much of what is written is fiction, if not downright black art."

"But the book I read was sent me by the mighty emperor of Japan," said the emperor. "Therefore it can't be a pack of lies. I must hear this nightingale. I insist upon his being here this evening. He has my highest imperial favor, and if he is not forthcoming I will have the whole court punched in the stomach, directly after supper."

"Tsing-pe!" said the lord-in-waiting, and off he scurried up the stairs, through all the rooms and corridors. And half the court ran with him, for no one wanted to be punched in the stomach after supper.

There was much questioning as to the whereabouts of this remarkable nightingale, who was so well known everywhere in the world except at home. At last they found a poor little kitchen girl, who said:

"The nightingale? I know him well. Yes, indeed he can sing. Every evening I get leave to carry scraps from the table to my sick mother. She lives down by the shore. When I start back I am tired, and rest in the woods. Then I hear the nightingale sing. It brings tears to my eyes. It's as if my mother were kissing me."

"Little kitchen girl," said the lord-in-waiting, "I'll have you appointed scullion for life. I'll even get permission for you to watch the emperor dine, if you'll take us to the nightingale who is commanded to appear at court this evening."

So they went into the forest where the nightingale usually sang. Half the court went along. On the way to the forest a cow began to moo.

"Oh," cried a courtier, "that must be it. What a powerful voice for a creature so small. I'm sure I've heard her sing before."

"No, that's the cow lowing," said the little kitchen girl. "We still have a long way to go."

Then the frogs in the marsh began to croak.

"Glorious!" said the Chinese court parson. "Now I hear it—like church bells ringing."

"No, that's the frogs," said the little kitchen girl. "But I think we shall hear him soon."

Then the nightingale sang.

"That's it," said the little kitchen girl. "Listen, listen! And yonder he sits." She pointed to a little gray bird high up in the branches.

"Is it possible?" cried the lord-in-waiting. "Well, I never would have thought he looked like that, so unassuming. But he has probably turned pale at seeing so many important people around him."

"Little nightingale," the kitchen girl called to him, "our gracious emperor wants to hear you sing."

"With the greatest of pleasure," answered the nightingale, and burst into song.

"Very similar to the sound of glass bells," said the lord-in-waiting. "Just see his little throat, how busily it throbs. I'm astounded that we have never heard him before. I'm sure he'll be a great success at court."

"Shall I sing to the emperor again?" asked the nightingale, for he thought that the emperor was present.

"My good little nightingale," said the lord-in-waiting, "I have the honor to command your presence at a court function this evening, where you'll delight His Majesty the Emperor with your charming song."

"My song sounds best in the woods," said the nightingale, but he went with them willingly when he heard it was the emperor's wish.

The palace had been especially polished for the occasion. The porcelain walls and floors shone in the rays of many gold lamps. The flowers with tinkling bells on them had been brought into the halls, and there was such a commotion of coming and going that all the bells chimed away until you could scarcely hear yourself talk.

In the middle of the great throne room, where the emperor sat, there was a golden perch for the nightingale. The whole court was there, and they let the little kitchen girl stand behind the door, now that she had been appointed "Imperial Pot Walloper." Everyone was dressed in his best, and all stared at the little gray bird to which the emperor graciously nodded.

And the nightingale sang so sweetly that tears came into the emperor's eyes and rolled down his cheeks. Then the nightingale sang still more sweetly, and it was the emperor's heart that melted. The emperor

Unquestionably the nightingale was a success.
He was to stay at court, and have his own cage.

was so touched that he wanted his own golden slipper hung around the nightingale's neck, but the nightingale declined it with thanks. He had already been amply rewarded.

"I have seen tears in the emperor's eyes," he said. "Nothing could surpass that. An emperor's tears are strangely powerful. I have my reward." And he sang again, gloriously.

"It's the most charming coquetry we ever heard," said the ladies-in-waiting. And they took water in their mouths so they could gurgle when anyone spoke to them, hoping to rival the nightingale. Even the lackeys and chambermaids said they were satisfied, which was saying a great deal, for they were the hardest to please. Unquestionably the nightingale was a success. He was to stay at court, and have his own cage. He had permission to go for a walk twice a day, and once at night. Twelve footmen attended him, each one holding tight to a ribbon tied to the bird's leg. There wasn't much fun in such outings.

The whole town talked about the marvelous bird, and if two people met, one could scarcely say "night" before the other said "gale," and then they would sigh in unison, with no need for words. Eleven pork butchers' children were named "Nightingale," but not one could sing.

One day the emperor received a large package labeled "The Nightingale."

"This must be another book about my celebrated bird," he said. But it was not a book. In the box was a work of art, an artificial nightingale most like the real one except that it was encrusted with diamonds, rubies, and sapphires. When it was wound, the artificial bird could sing one of the nightingale's songs while it wagged its glittering gold and silver tail. Round its neck hung a ribbon inscribed:"The emperor of Japan's nightingale is a poor thing compared with that of the emperor of China."

"Isn't that nice?" everyone said, and the man who had brought the contraption was immediately promoted to be "Imperial Nightingale Fetcher in Chief."

Where was he?
No one had noticed him flying out the open window,
back to his home in the green forest.

"Now let's have them sing together. What a duet that will be," said the courtiers.

So they had to sing together, but it didn't turn out so well, for the real nightingale sang whatever came into his head while the imitation bird sang by rote.

"That's not the newcomer's fault," said the music master. "He keeps perfect time, just as I have taught him."

Then they had the imitation bird sing by itself. It met with the same success as the real nightingale, and besides it was much prettier to see, all sparkling like bracelets and breastpins. Three and thirty times it sang the selfsame song without tiring. The courtiers would gladly have heard it again, but the emperor said the real nightingale should now have his turn. Where was he? No one had noticed him flying out the open window, back to his home in the green forest.

"But what made him do that?" said the emperor.

All the courtiers slandered the nightingale, whom they called a most ungrateful wretch. "Luckily we have the best bird," they said, and made the imitation one sing again. That was the thirty-fourth time they had heard the same tune, but they didn't quite know it by heart because it was a difficult piece. And the music master praised the artificial bird beyond measure. Yes, he said that the contraption was much better than the real nightingale, not only in its dress and its many beautiful diamonds, but also in its mechanical interior.

"You see, ladies and gentlemen, and above all Your Imperial Majesty, with a real nightingale one never knows what to expect, but with this artificial bird everything goes according to plan. Nothing is left to chance. I can explain it and take it to pieces, and show how the mechanical wheels are arranged, how they go around, and how one follows after another."

"Those are our sentiments exactly," they all said, and the music master was commanded to have the bird give a public concert next Sunday. The

emperor said that his people should hear it. And hear it they did, with as much pleasure as if they had all gotten tipsy on tea, Chinese fashion. Everyone said, "Oh," and held up the finger we call "lickpot," and nodded his head. But the poor fisherman who had heard the real nightingale said, "This is very pretty, very nearly the real thing, but not quite. I can't imagine what's lacking."

The real nightingale had been banished from the land. In its place, the artificial bird sat on a cushion beside the emperor's bed. All its gold and jeweled presents lay about it, and its title was now "Grand Imperial Singer of the Emperor to Sleep." In rank it stood first from the left, for the emperor gave pre-eminence to the left side because of the heart. Even an emperor's heart is on the left.

The music master wrote a twenty-five-volume book about the artificial bird. It was learned, long-winded, and full of hard Chinese words, yet everybody said they had read and understood it, lest they show themselves stupid and would then have been punched in their stomachs.

After a year the emperor, his court, and all the other Chinamen knew every twitter of the artificial song by heart. They liked it all the better now that they could sing it themselves. Which they did. The street urchins sang, "Zizizi! Kluk, kluk, kluk," and the emperor sang it, too. That's how popular it was.

But one night, while the artificial bird was singing his best by the emperor's bed, something inside the bird broke with a twang. *Whir-r-r,* all the wheels ran down and the music stopped. Out of bed jumped the emperor and sent for his own physician, but what could he do? Then he sent for a watchmaker, who conferred, and investigated, and patched up the bird after a fashion. But the watchmaker said that the bird must be spared too much exertion, for the cogs were badly worn and if he replaced them it would spoil the tune. This was terrible. Only once a year could they let the bird sing, and that was almost too much for it.

But the music master made a little speech full of hard Chinese words that meant that the bird was as good as it ever was. So that made it as good as ever.

Five years passed by, and a real sorrow befell the whole country. The Chinamen loved their emperor, and now he fell ill. Ill unto death, it was said. A new emperor was chosen in readiness. People stood in the palace street and asked the lord-in-waiting how it went with their emperor.

"P," said he, and shook his head.

Cold and pale lay the emperor in his great, magnificent bed. All the courtiers thought he was dead, and went to do homage to the new emperor. The lackeys went off to trade gossip, and the chambermaids gave a coffee party because it was such a special occasion. Deep mats were laid in all the rooms and passageways, to muffle each footstep. It was quiet in the palace, dead quiet. But the emperor was not yet dead. Stiff and pale he lay, in his magnificent bed with the long velvet curtains and the heavy gold tassels. High in the wall was an open window, through which moonlight fell on the emperor and his artificial bird.

The poor emperor could hardly breathe. It was as if something were sitting on his chest. Opening his eyes he saw it was Death who sat there, wearing the emperor's crown, handling the emperor's gold sword, and carrying the emperor's silk banner. Among the folds of the great velvet curtains there were strangely familiar faces. Some were horrible, others gentle and kind. They were the emperor's deeds, good and bad, who came back to him now that Death sat on his heart.

"Don't you remember—?" they whispered one after the other. "Don't you remember—?" And they told him of things that made the cold sweat run on his forehead.

"No, I will not remember!" said the emperor. "Music, music, sound the great drum of China lest I hear what they say!" But they went on whispering, and Death nodded, Chinese fashion, at every word.

The poor emperor could hardly breathe.
It was as if something were sitting on his chest.
Opening his eyes he saw it was Death.

"Music, music!" the emperor called. "Sing, my precious little golden bird, sing! I have given you gold and precious presents. I have hung my golden slipper around your neck. Sing, I pray you, sing!"

But the bird stood silent. There was no one to wind it, nothing to make it sing. Death kept staring through his great hollow eyes, and it was quiet, deadly quiet.

Suddenly, through the window came a burst of song. It was the little live nightingale, who sat outside on a spray. He had heard the emperor's plight, and had come to sing of comfort and hope. As he sang, the phantoms grew pale, and still more pale, and the blood flowed quicker and quicker through the emperor's feeble body. Even Death listened, and said, "Go on, little nightingale, go on!"

"But," said the little nightingale, "will you give back that sword, that banner, that emperor's crown?"

And Death gave back these treasures for a song. The nightingale sang on. It sang of the quiet churchyard where white roses grow, where the elder-flowers make the air sweet, and where the grass is always green, wet with the tears of those who are still alive. Death longed for his grand garden. Out through the windows drifted a cold gray mist, as Death departed.

"Thank you, thank you!" the emperor said. "Little bird from Heaven, I know you of old. I banished you once from my land, and yet you have sung away the evil faces from my bed, and Death from my heart. How can I repay you?"

"You have already rewarded me," said the nightingale. "I brought tears to your eyes when first I sang for you. To the heart of a singer those are more precious than any precious stone. But sleep now, and grow fresh and strong while I sing." He sang on until the emperor fell into a sound, refreshing sleep, a sweet and soothing slumber.

The sun was shining in his window when the emperor awoke, restored and well. Not one of his servants had returned to him, for they thought him dead, but the nightingale still sang.

"You must stay with me always," said the emperor. "Sing to me only when you please. I shall break the artificial bird into a thousand pieces."

"No," said the nightingale. "It did its best. Keep it near you. I cannot build my nest here, or live in a palace, so let me come as I will. Then I shall sit on the spray by your window, and sing things that will make you happy and thoughtful, too. I'll sing about those who are gay, and those who are sorrowful. My songs will tell you of all the good and evil that you do not see. A little singing bird flies far and wide, to the fisherman's hut, to the farmer's house, and to many other places a long way off from you and your court. I love your heart better than I do your crown, and yet the crown has been blessed, too. I will come and sing to you, if you will promise me one thing."

"All that I have is yours," cried the emperor, who stood in his imperial robes, which he had put on himself, and held his heavy gold sword to his heart.

"One thing only," the nightingale asked. "You must not let anyone know that you have a little bird who tells you everything; then all will go even better." And away he flew.

The servants came in to look after their dead emperor—and there they stood. And the emperor said, "Good morning."

"I love your heart better than I do your crown,"
said the nightingale,
"and yet the crown has been blessed, too."

The Little Mermaid

Semi-human life forms—whether in the sky, the earth, or under water—have long been the subject of legend. In the Romantic culture that infused Andersen's era, water spirits like merfolk were particularly popular. This interest, mixed with a dose of Victorian sentimentalism and self-restraint, is a hallmark of Andersen's soaring story about a mermaid who pays a heavy price for loving a prince. The 1837 tale made him world-famous and remains one of his best known. Some have criticized him for the mermaid's suffering and self-sacrifice, but emotional pain was no stranger to Andersen, who wrote to a friend: "I suffer with my characters." Biographer Jackie Wullschlager suggests that as Andersen failed in love—a source of great disappointment, which has led historians to see the story as partially autobiographical—he began to see his writing, not everlasting love, as the source of his own immortality. His tale was inspired by Friedrich de la Motte Fouqué's *Undine* (1811), but unlike Fouqué's, Andersen's mermaid does not acquire an immortal soul through love. In a letter Andersen shared, "I *won't* accept this sort of thing in this world," expressing his heartfelt conviction that redemption shouldn't be contingent on whether one finds love.—ND

Watercolors by Josef Paleček, Czech, 1981
and paper cuts by Lotte Reiniger, German, 1980

From the deepest spot in the ocean rises
the palace of the sea king,
with walls of coral and windows of amber.

ar out in the ocean the water is as blue as the petals of the loveliest cornflower, and as clear as the purest glass. But it is very deep, too. It goes down deeper than any anchor rope will go, and many, many steeples would have to be stacked one on top of another to reach from the bottom to the surface of the sea. It is down there that the sea folk live.

Now don't suppose that there are only bare white sands at the bottom of the sea. No indeed! The most marvelous trees and flowers grow down there, with such pliant stalks and leaves that the least stir in the water makes them move about as though they were alive. All sorts of fish, large and small, dart among the branches, just as birds flit through the trees up here. From the deepest spot in the ocean rises the palace of the sea king. Its walls are made of coral and its high pointed windows of the clearest amber, and the roof is made of mussel shells that open and shut with the tide. This is a wonderful sight to see, for every shell holds glistening pearls, any one of which would be the pride of a queen's crown.

The sea king down there had been a widower for years, and his old mother kept house for him. She was a clever woman, but very proud of her noble birth. Therefore she flaunted twelve oysters on her tail while the other ladies of the court were only allowed to wear six. Except for this she was an altogether praiseworthy person, particularly so because she was extremely fond of her granddaughters, the little sea princesses. They were six lovely girls, but the youngest was the most beautiful of them all. Her skin was as soft and tender as a rose petal, and her eyes were as blue as the deep sea, but like all the others she had no feet. Her body ended in a fish tail.

The whole day long they used to play in the palace, down in the great halls where live flowers grew on the walls. Whenever the high amber windows were thrown open the fish would swim in, just as swallows dart

*The figure of a handsome boy had sunk down
from a shipwreck. Beside the statue the little mermaid
planted a weeping willow tree.*

into our rooms when we open the windows. But these fish, now, would swim right up to the little princesses to eat out of their hands and let themselves be petted.

Outside the palace was a big garden, with flaming red and deep-blue trees. Their fruit glittered like gold, and their blossoms flamed like fire on their constantly waving stalks. The soil was very fine sand indeed, but as blue as burning brimstone. A strange blue veil lay over everything down there. You would have thought yourself aloft in the air with only the blue sky above and beneath you, rather than down at the bottom of the sea. When there was a dead calm, you could just see the sun, like a scarlet flower with light streaming from its calyx.

Each little princess had her own small garden plot, where she could dig and plant whatever she liked. One of them made her little flower bed in the shape of a whale, another thought it neater to shape hers like a little mermaid, but the youngest of them made hers as round as the sun, and there she grew only flowers that were as red as the sun itself. She was an unusual child, quiet and wistful, and when her sisters decorated their gardens with all kinds of odd things they had found in sunken ships, she would allow nothing in hers except flowers as red as the sun, and a pretty marble statue. This figure of a handsome boy, carved in pure white marble, had sunk down to the bottom of the sea from some ship that was wrecked. Beside the statue she planted a rose-colored weeping willow tree, which thrived so well that its graceful branches shaded

the statue and hung down to the blue sand, where their shadows took on a violet tint, and swayed as the branches swayed. It looked as if the roots and the tips of the branches were kissing each other in play.

Nothing gave the youngest princess such pleasure as to hear about the world of human beings up above them. Her old grandmother had to tell her all she knew about ships and cities, and of people and animals. What seemed nicest of all to her was that up on land the flowers were fragrant, for those at the bottom of the sea had no scent. And she thought it was nice that the woods were green, and that the fish you saw among their branches could sing so loud and sweet that it was delightful to hear them. Her grandmother had to call the little birds "fish," or the princess would not have known what she was talking about, for she had never seen a bird.

"When you get to be fifteen," her grandmother said, "you will be allowed to rise up out of the ocean and sit on the rocks in the moonlight, to watch the great ships sailing by. You will see woods and towns, too."

Next year one of her sisters would be fifteen, but the others—well, since each was a whole year older than the next the youngest still had five long years to wait until she could rise up from the water and see what our world was like. But each sister promised to tell the others about all that she saw, and what she found most marvelous on her first day. Their grandmother had not told them half enough, and there were so many things that they longed to know about.

The most eager of them all was the youngest, the very one who was so quiet and wistful. Many a night she stood by her open window and looked up through the dark blue water where the fish waved their fins and tails. She could just see the moon and stars. To be sure, their light was quite dim, but looked at through the water they seemed much bigger than they appear to us. Whenever a cloudlike shadow swept across them, she knew that it was either a whale swimming overhead, or a ship with

On many an evening the older sisters would rise
to the surface, arm in arm, all five in a row.

many human beings aboard it. Little did they dream that a pretty young mermaid was down below, stretching her white arms up toward the keel of their ship.

The eldest princess had her fifteenth birthday, so now she received permission to rise up out of the water. When she came back she had a hundred things to tell her sisters about, but the most marvelous thing of all, she said, was to lie on a sandbar in the moonlight, when the sea was calm, and to gaze at the large city on the shore, where the lights twinkled like hundreds of stars; to listen to music; to hear the clatter and clamor of carriages and people; to see so many church towers and spires; and to hear the ringing bells. Because she could not enter the city, that was just what she most dearly longed to do.

Oh, how intently the youngest sister listened. After this, whenever she stood at her open window at night and looked up through the dark blue waters, she thought of that great city with all of its clatter and clamor, and even fancied that in these depths she could hear the church bells ring.

The next year, her second sister had permission to rise up to the surface and swim wherever she pleased. She came up just at sunset, and she said that this spectacle was the most marvelous sight she had ever seen. The heavens had a golden glow, and as for the clouds—she could not find words to describe their beauty. Splashed with red and tinted with violet, they sailed over her head. But much faster than the sailing clouds were wild swans in a flock. Like a long white veil trailing above the sea, they flew toward the setting sun. She too swam toward it, but down it went, and all the rose-colored glow faded from the sea and sky.

The following year, her third sister ascended, and as she was the boldest of them all she swam up a broad river that flowed into the ocean. She saw gloriously green, vine-colored hills. Palaces and manor houses could be glimpsed through the splendid woods. She heard all the birds

The sun had just gone down,
but the clouds still shone like gold and roses.
A great three-master lay in view.

sing, and the sun shone so brightly that often she had to dive under the water to cool her burning face. In a small cove she found a whole school of mortal children, paddling about in the water quite naked. She wanted to play with them, but they took fright and ran away. Then along came a little black animal—it was a dog, but she had never seen a dog before. It barked so ferociously that she took fright herself, and fled to the open sea. But never could she forget the splendid woods, the green hills, and the nice children who could swim in the water although they didn't wear fish tails.

The fourth sister was not so venturesome. She stayed far out among the rough waves, which she said was a marvelous place. You could see all around you for miles and miles, and the heavens up above you were like a vast dome of glass. She had seen ships, but they were so far away that they looked like seagulls. Playful dolphins had turned somersaults, and monstrous whales had spouted water through their blowholes so that it looked as if hundreds of fountains were playing all around them.

Now the fifth sister had her turn. Her birthday came in the wintertime, so she saw things that none of the others had seen. The sea was a deep green color, and enormous icebergs drifted about. Each one glistened like a pearl, she said, but they were more lofty than any church steeple built by man. They assumed the most fantastic shapes, and sparkled like diamonds. She had seated herself on the largest one, and all the ships that came sailing by sped away as soon as the frightened sailors saw her there with her long hair blowing in the wind.

In the late evening clouds filled the sky. Thunder cracked and lightning darted across the heavens. Black waves lifted those great bergs of ice on high, where they flashed when the lightning struck.

On all the ships the sails were reefed and there was fear and trembling. But quietly she sat there, upon her drifting iceberg, and watched the blue forked lightning strike the sea.

Each of the sisters took delight in the lovely new sights when she first rose up to the surface of the sea. But when they became grown-up girls, who were allowed to go wherever they liked, they became indifferent to it. They would become homesick, and in a month they said that there was no place like the bottom of the sea, where they felt so completely at home.

On many an evening the older sisters would rise to the surface, arm in arm, all five in a row. They had beautiful voices, more charming than those of any mortal beings. When a storm was brewing, and they anticipated a shipwreck, they would swim before the ship and sing most seductively of how beautiful it was at the bottom of the ocean, trying to overcome the prejudice that the sailors had against coming down to them. But people could not understand their song, and mistook it for the voice of the storm. Nor was it for them to see the glories of the deep. When their ship went down they were drowned, and it was as dead men that they reached the sea king's palace.

On the evenings when the mermaids rose through the water like this, arm in arm, their youngest sister stayed behind all alone, looking after them and wanting to weep. But a mermaid has no tears, and therefore she suffers so much more.

"Oh, how I do wish I were fifteen!" she said. "I know I shall love that world up there and all the people who live in it."

And at last she too came to be fifteen.

"Now I'll have you off my hands," said her grandmother, the old queen dowager. "Come, let me adorn you like your sisters." In the little maid's hair she put a wreath of white lilies, each petal of which was formed from half of a pearl. And the old queen let eight big oysters fasten themselves to the princess's tail, as a sign of her high rank.

"But that hurts!" said the little mermaid.

"You must put up with a good deal to keep up appearances," her grandmother told her.

Oh, how gladly she would have shaken off all these decorations, and laid aside the cumbersome wreath! The red flowers in her garden were much more becoming to her, but she didn't dare to make any changes. "Goodbye," she said, and up she went through the water, as light and as sparkling as a bubble.

The sun had just gone down when her head rose above the surface, but the clouds still shone like gold and roses, and in the delicately tinted sky sparkled the clear gleam of the evening star. The air was mild and fresh and the sea unruffled. A great three-master lay in view with only one of all its sails set, for there was not even the whisper of a breeze, and the sailors idled about in the rigging and on the yards. There was music and singing on the ship, and as night came on they lighted hundreds of such brightly colored lanterns that one might have thought the flags of all nations were swinging in the air.

The little mermaid swam right up to the window of the main cabin, and each time she rose with the swell she could peep in through the clear glass panes at the crowd of brilliantly dressed people within. The handsomest of them all was a young prince with big dark eyes. He could not be more than sixteen years old. It was his birthday and that was the reason for all the celebration. Up on deck the sailors were dancing, and when the prince appeared among them a hundred or more rockets flew through the air, making it as bright as day. These startled the little mermaid so badly that she ducked under the water. But she soon peeped up again, and then it seemed as if all the stars in the sky were falling around her. Never had she seen such fireworks. Great suns spun around, splendid fire-fish floated through the blue air, and all these things were mirrored in the crystal-clear sea. It was so brilliantly bright that you could see every little rope of the ship, and the people could be seen distinctly. Oh, how handsome the young prince was! He laughed, and he smiled and shook people by the hand, while the music rang out in the perfect evening.

His beautiful eyes were closing,
and he would have died if the mermaid had not
come to help. She held his head above water.

It got very late, but the little mermaid could not take her eyes off the ship and the handsome prince. The brightly colored lanterns were put out, no more rockets flew through the air, and no more cannon boomed. But there was a mutter and rumble deep down in the sea, and the swell kept bouncing her up so high that she could look into the cabin.

Now the ship began to sail. Canvas after canvas was spread in the wind, the waves rose high, great clouds gathered, and lightning flashed in the distance. Ah, they were in for a terrible storm, and the mariners made haste to reef the sails. The tall ship pitched and rolled as it sped through the angry sea. The waves rose up like towering black mountains, as if they would break over the masthead, but the swanlike ship plunged into the valleys between such waves, and emerged to ride their lofty heights. To the little mermaid this seemed good sport, but to the sailors it was nothing of the sort. The ship creaked and labored, thick timbers gave way under the heavy blows, waves broke over the ship, the mainmast snapped in two like a reed, the ship listed over on its side, and water burst into the hold.

Now the little mermaid saw that people were in peril, and that she herself must take care to avoid the beams and wreckage tossed about by the sea. One moment it would be black as pitch, and she couldn't see a thing. Next moment the lightning would flash so brightly that she could distinguish every soul on board. Everyone was looking out for himself as best he could. She watched closely for the young prince, and when the ship split in two she saw him sink down in the sea. At first she was overjoyed that he would be with her, but then she recalled that human people could not live under the water, and he could only visit her father's palace as a dead man. No, he should not die! So she swam in among all the floating planks and beams, completely forgetting that they might crush her. She dived through the waves and rode their crests, until at length she reached the young prince, who was no longer able to swim in the raging sea. His arms and legs were exhausted, his beautiful eyes were closing, and he would have died if the little mermaid had not come to help him. She held his head above water, and let the waves take them wherever the waves went.

At daybreak, when the storm was over, not a trace of the ship was in view. The sun rose out of the water, red and bright, and its beams seemed to bring the glow of life back to the cheeks of the prince, but his eyes remained closed. The mermaid kissed his high and shapely forehead. As she stroked his wet hair into place, it seemed to her that he looked like that marble statue in her little garden. She kissed him again and hoped that he would live.

She saw dry land rise before her in high blue mountains, topped with snow as glistening white as if a flock of swans were resting there. Down by the shore were splendid green woods, and in the foreground stood a church, or perhaps a convent; she didn't know which, but anyway it was a building. Orange and lemon trees grew in its garden, and tall palm trees grew beside the gateway. Here the sea formed a little harbor, quite calm and very deep. Fine white sand had been washed up below the cliffs. She swam there with the handsome prince, and stretched him out on the sand, taking special care to pillow his head up high in the warm sunlight.

The bells began to ring in the great white building, and a number of young girls came out into the garden. The little mermaid swam away behind some tall rocks that stuck out of the water. She covered her hair and her shoulders with foam so that no one could see her tiny face, and then she watched to see who would find the poor prince.

In a little while one of the young girls came upon him. She seemed frightened, but only for a minute; then she called more people. The mermaid watched the prince regain consciousness, and smile at everyone around him. But he did not smile at her, for he did not even know that she had saved him. She felt very unhappy, and when they led him away

Finally she couldn't bear it any longer.
She told her secret to one of her sisters.
Immediately all the other sisters heard about it.

to the big building she dived sadly down into the water and returned to her father's palace.

She had always been quiet and wistful, and now she became much more so. Her sisters asked her what she had seen on her first visit up to the surface, but she would not tell them a thing.

Many evenings and many mornings she revisited the spot where she had left the prince. She saw the

fruit in the garden ripened and harvested, and she saw the snow on the high mountain melted away, but she did not see the prince, so each time she came home sadder than she had left. It was her one consolation to sit in her little garden and throw her arms about the beautiful marble statue that looked so much like the prince. But she took no care of her flowers now. They overgrew the paths until the place was a wilderness, and their long stalks and leaves became so entangled in the branches of the tree that it cast a gloomy shade.

Finally she couldn't bear it any longer. She told her secret to one of her sisters. Immediately all the other sisters heard about it. No one else knew, except a few more mermaids who told no one—except their most intimate friends. One of these friends knew who the prince was. She too had seen the birthday celebration on the ship. She knew where he came from and where his kingdom was.

"Come, little sister!" said the other princesses. Arm in arm, they rose from the water in a long row, right in front of where they knew the prince's palace stood. It was built of pale, glistening, golden stone with great marble staircases, one of which led down to the sea. Magnificent gilt domes rose above the roof, and between the pillars all around the buildings were marble statues that looked most lifelike. Through the clear glass of the lofty windows one could see into the splendid halls, with their costly silk hangings and tapestries, and walls covered with paintings that were delightful to behold. In the center of the main hall a large fountain played its columns of spray up to the glass-domed roof, through which the sun shone down on the water and upon the lovely plants that grew in the big basin.

Now that she knew where he lived, many an evening and many a night she spent there in the sea. She swam much closer to shore than any of her sisters would dare venture, and she even went far up a narrow stream, under the splendid marble balcony that cast its long shadow in the water. Here she used to sit and watch the young prince when he thought himself quite alone in the bright moonlight.

On many evenings she saw him sail out in his fine boat, with music playing and flags aflutter. She would peep out through the green rushes, and if the wind blew her long silver veil, anyone who saw it mistook it for a swan spreading its wings.

On many nights she saw the fishermen come out to sea with their torches, and heard them tell about how kind the young prince was. This made her proud to think that it was she who had saved his life when he was buffeted about, half dead among the waves. And she thought of how softly his head had rested on her breast, and how tenderly she had kissed him, though he knew nothing of all this nor could he even dream of it.

Increasingly she grew to like human beings, and more and more she longed to live among them. Their world seemed so much wider than her own, for they could skim over the sea in ships, and mount up into the lofty peaks high over the clouds, and their lands stretched out in woods and fields farther than the eye could see. There was so much she wanted

"Why weren't we given an immortal soul?"
the little mermaid sadly asked.
"You must not think about that," said the old lady.

to know. Her sisters could not answer all her questions, so she asked her old grandmother, who knew about the "upper world," which was what she said was the right name for the countries above the sea.

"If men aren't drowned," the little mermaid asked, "do they live on forever? Don't they die, as we do down here in the sea?"

"Yes," the old lady said, "they too must die, and their lifetimes are even shorter than ours. We can live to be three hundred years old, but when we perish we turn into mere foam on the sea, and haven't even a grave down here among our dear ones. We have no immortal soul, no life hereafter. We are like the green seaweed—once cut down, it never grows again. Human beings, on the contrary, have a soul that lives forever, long after their bodies have turned to clay. It rises through thin air, up to the shining stars. Just as we rise through the water to see the lands on earth, so men rise up to beautiful places unknown, which we shall never see."

"Why weren't we given an immortal soul?" the little mermaid sadly asked. "I would gladly give up my three hundred years if I could be a human being only for a day, and later share in that heavenly realm."

"You must not think about that," said the old lady. "We fare much more happily and are much better off than the folk up there."

"Then I must also die and float as foam upon the sea, not hearing the music of the waves, and seeing neither the beautiful flowers nor the red sun! Can't I do anything at all to win an immortal soul?"

She saw that every polyp held something
it had caught—the white bones of men, ships' rudders,
seamen's chests, the skeletons of animals.

"No," her grandmother answered, "not unless a human being loved you so much that you meant more to him than his father and mother. If his every thought and his whole heart cleaved to you so that he would let a priest join his right hand to yours and would promise to be faithful here and throughout all eternity, then his soul would dwell in your body, and you would share in the happiness of mankind. He would give you a soul and yet keep his own. But that can never come to pass. The very thing that is your greatest beauty here in the sea—your fish tail—would be considered ugly on land. They have such poor taste that to be thought beautiful there you have to have two awkward props which they call legs."

The little mermaid sighed and looked unhappily at her fish tail.

"Come, let us be gay!" the old lady said. "Let us leap and bound throughout the three hundred years that we have to live. Surely that is time and to spare, and afterwards we shall be glad enough to rest in our graves. We are holding a court ball this evening."

This was a much more glorious affair than is ever to be seen on earth. The walls and the ceiling of the great ballroom were made of massive but transparent glass. Many hundreds of huge rose-red and grass-green shells stood on each side in rows, with the blue flames that burned in each shell illuminating the whole room and shining through the walls so clearly that it was quite bright in the sea outside. You could see the countless fish, great and small, swimming toward the glass walls. On some of them the scales gleamed purplish-red, while others were silver and gold. Across the floor of the hall ran a wide stream of water, and upon this the mermaids and mermen danced to their own entrancing songs. Such beautiful voices are not to be heard among the people who live on land. The little mermaid sang more sweetly than anyone else, and everyone applauded her. For a moment her heart was happy, because she knew she had the loveliest voice of all, in the sea or on the land. But her thoughts soon strayed to the world up above. She could not forget the charming prince, nor her sorrow that she did not have an immortal soul like his. Therefore she stole out of her father's palace and, while everything there was song and gladness, she sat sadly in her own little garden.

Then she heard a bugle call through the water, and she thought, "That must mean he is sailing up there, he whom I love more than my father or mother, he of whom I am always thinking, and in whose hands I would so willingly trust my lifelong happiness. I dare do anything to win him and gain an immortal soul. While my sisters are dancing here, in my father's palace, I shall visit the sea witch of whom I have always been so afraid. Perhaps she will be able to advise me and help me."

The little mermaid set out from her garden toward the whirlpools that raged in front of the witch's dwelling. She had never gone that way before. No flowers grew there, nor any seaweed. Bare and gray, the sands extended to the whirlpools, where like roaring mill wheels the waters whirled and snatched everything within their reach down to the bottom of the sea. Between these tumultuous whirlpools she had to thread her way to reach the witch's waters, and then for a long stretch the only trail lay through a hot, seething mire, which the witch called her peat marsh. Beyond it her house lay in the middle of a weird forest, where all the trees and shrubs were polyps, half animal and half plant. They looked like hundred-headed snakes growing out of the soil. All their branches were long, slimy arms, with fingers like wriggling worms. They squirmed, joint by joint, from their roots to their outermost tentacles, and whatever they could lay hold of they twined around and never let go. The little mermaid was terrified, and stopped at the edge of the forest. Her heart thumped with fear and she nearly turned back, but then she remembered the prince and the souls that men have, and she summoned her courage. She bound her long flowing locks closely about her head so that the polyps could not catch hold of them, folded her arms across her breast, and darted through the water like a fish, in among the slimy polyps that stretched out their writhing arms and fingers to seize her. She saw that every one of them held something that it had caught with its hundreds of little tentacles, and to which it clung as with strong hoops of steel. The white bones of men who had perished at sea and sunk to these depths could be seen in the polyps' arms. Ships' rudders, and seamen's chests, and the skeletons of land animals had also fallen into their clutches, but the most ghastly sight of all was a little mermaid whom they had caught and strangled.

She reached a large muddy clearing in the forest, where big fat water snakes slithered about, showing their foul yellowish bellies. In the middle of this clearing was a house built of the bones of shipwrecked men, and there sat the sea witch, letting a toad eat out of her mouth just as we might feed sugar to a little canary bird. She called the ugly fat water snakes her little chicabiddies, and let them crawl and sprawl about on her spongy bosom.

"I know exactly what you want," said the sea witch. "It is very foolish of you, but just the same you shall have your way, for it will bring you to grief, my proud princess. You want to get rid of your fish tail and have two props instead, so that you can walk about like a human creature, and have the young prince fall in love with you, and win him and an immortal soul besides." At this, the witch gave such a loud cackling laugh that the toad and the snakes were shaken to the ground, where they lay writhing.

"You are just in time," said the witch. "After the sun comes up tomorrow, a whole year would have to go by before I could be of any help to you. I shall compound you a draft, and before sunrise you must swim to shore with it, seat yourself on dry land, and drink the draft down. Then your tail will divide and shrink until it becomes what the people on earth call a pair of shapely legs. But it will hurt; it will feel as if a sharp sword

The witch said,
"I will take the very best thing that you have
—your sweet voice—in return for my draft."

slashed through you. Everyone who sees you will say that you are the most graceful human being they have ever laid eyes on, for you will keep your gliding movement and no dancer will be able to tread as lightly as you. But every step you take will feel as if you were treading upon knife blades so sharp that blood must flow. I am willing to help you, but are you willing to suffer all this?"

"Yes," the little mermaid said in a trembling voice, as she thought of the prince and of gaining a human soul.

"Remember!" said the witch. "Once you have taken a human form, you can never be a mermaid again. You can never come back through the waters to your sisters, or to your father's palace. And if you do not win the love of the prince so completely that for your sake he forgets his father and mother, cleaves to you with his every thought and his whole heart, and lets the priest join your hands in marriage, then you will win no immortal soul. If he marries someone else, your heart will break on the very next morning, and you will become foam of the sea."

"I shall take that risk," said the little mermaid, but she turned as pale as death.

"Also, you will have to pay me," said the witch, "and it is no trifling price that I'm asking. You have the sweetest voice of anyone down here at the bottom of the sea, and while I don't doubt that you would like to captivate the prince with it, you must give this voice to me. I will take the very best thing that you have, in return for my sovereign draft. I must pour my own blood in it to make the drink as sharp as a two-edged sword."

"But if you take my voice," said the little mermaid, "what will be left to me?"

"Your lovely form," the witch told her, "your gliding movements, and your eloquent eyes. With these you can easily enchant a human heart. Well, have you lost your courage? Stick out your little tongue and I shall

She charmed everyone, and danced time and again,
though every time she touched the floor
she felt as if she were treading on sharp-edged steel.

cut it off. I'll have my price, and you shall have the potent draft."

"Go ahead," said the little mermaid.

The witch hung her cauldron over the flames, to brew the draft. "Cleanliness is a good thing," she said, as she tied her snakes in a knot and scoured out the pot with them. Then she pricked herself in the chest and let her black blood splash into the cauldron. Steam swirled up from it, in such ghastly shapes that anyone would have been terrified by them. The witch constantly threw new ingredients into the cauldron, and it started to boil with a sound like that of a crocodile shedding tears. When the draft was ready at last, it looked as clear as the purest water.

"There's your draft," said the witch. And she cut off the tongue of the little mermaid, who now was dumb and could neither sing nor talk.

"If the polyps should pounce on you when you walk back through my wood," the witch said, "just spill a drop of this brew upon them and their tentacles will break in a thousand pieces." But there was no need of that, for the polyps curled up in terror as soon as they saw the bright draft. It glittered in the little mermaid's hand as if it were a shining star. So she soon traversed the forest, the marsh, and the place of raging whirlpools.

She could see her father's palace. The lights had been snuffed out in the great ballroom, and doubtless everyone in the palace was asleep, but she dared not go near them, now that she was stricken dumb and was leaving her home forever. Her heart felt as if it would break with grief. She tiptoed into the garden, took one flower from each of her sisters' little plots, blew a thousand kisses toward the palace, and then mounted up through the dark blue sea.

The sun had not yet risen when she saw the prince's palace. As she climbed his splendid marble staircase, the moon was shining clear. The little mermaid swallowed the bitter, fiery draft, and it was as if a two-edged sword struck through her frail body. She swooned away, and lay there as if she were dead. When the sun rose over the sea she awoke and felt a flash of pain, but directly in front of her stood the handsome young prince, gazing at her with his coal-black eyes. Lowering her gaze, she saw that her fish tail was gone, and that she had the loveliest pair of white legs any young maid could hope to have. But she was naked, so she clothed herself in her own long hair.

The prince asked who she was, and how she came to be there. Her deep blue eyes looked at him tenderly but very sadly, for she could not speak. Then he took her hand and led her into his palace. Every footstep felt as if she were walking on the blades and points of sharp knives, just as the witch had foretold, but she gladly endured it. She moved as lightly as a bubble as she walked beside the prince. He and all who saw her marveled at the grace of her gliding walk.

Once clad in the rich silk and muslin garments that were provided for her, she was the loveliest person in all the palace, though she was dumb and could neither sing nor speak. Beautiful slaves, attired in silk and cloth of gold, came to sing before the prince and his royal parents. One of them sang more sweetly than all the others, and when the prince smiled at her and clapped his hands, the little mermaid felt very unhappy, for she knew that she herself used to sing much more sweetly.

"Oh," she thought, "if he only knew that I parted with my voice forever so that I could be near him."

Graceful slaves now began to dance to the most wonderful music. Then the little mermaid lifted her shapely white arms, rose up on the

She sat on the side of the ship gazing down.
Her sisters rose to the surface, looking at her sadly,
and wrung their hands.

tips of her toes, and skimmed over the floor. No one had ever danced so well. Each movement set off her beauty to better and better advantage, and her eyes spoke more directly to the heart than any of the singing slaves could do.

She charmed everyone, and especially the prince, who called her his dear little foundling. She danced time and again, though every time she touched the floor she felt as if she were treading on sharp-edged steel. The prince said he would keep her with him always, and that she was to have a velvet pillow to sleep on outside his door.

He had a page's suit made for her, so that she could go with him on horseback. They would ride through the sweet-scented woods, where the green boughs brushed her shoulders, and where the little birds sang among the fluttering leaves.

She climbed up high mountains with the prince, and though her tender feet bled so that all could see it, she only laughed and followed him on until they could see the clouds driving far below, like a flock of birds in flight to distant lands.

At home in the prince's palace, while the others slept at night, she would go down the broad marble steps to cool her burning feet in the cold sea-water, and then she would recall those who lived beneath the sea. One night her sisters came by, arm in arm, singing sadly as they breasted the waves. When she held out her hands toward them, they knew who she was and told her how unhappy she had made them all. They came to see her every night after that, and once far, far out to sea, she saw her old grandmother, who had not been up to the surface this many a year. With her was the sea king, with his crown upon his head. They stretched out their hands to her, but they did not venture so near the land as her sisters had.

Day after day she became more dear to the prince, who loved her as one would love a good little child, but he never thought of making her his

queen. Yet she had to be his wife or she would never have an immortal soul, and on the morning after his wedding she would turn into foam on the waves.

"Don't you love me best of all?" the little mermaid's eyes seemed to question him, when he took her in his arms and kissed her lovely forehead.

"Yes, you are most dear to me," said the prince, "for you have the kindest heart. You love me more than anyone else does, and you look so much like a young girl I once saw but shall never find again. I was on a ship that was wrecked and the waves cast me ashore near a holy temple, where many young girls performed the rituals. The youngest of them found me beside the sea and saved my life. Though I saw her no more than twice, she is the only person in all the world whom I could love. But you are so much like her that you almost replace the memory of her in my heart. She belongs to that holy temple, therefore it is my good fortune that I have you. We shall never part."

"Alas, he doesn't know it was I who saved his life," the little mermaid thought. "I carried him over the sea to the garden where the temple stands. I hid behind the foam and watched to see if anyone would come. I saw the pretty maid he loves better than me." A sigh was the only sign of her deep distress, for a mermaid cannot cry. "He says that the other maid belongs to the holy temple. She will never come out into the world, so they will never see each other again. It is I who will care for him, love him, and give all my life to him."

Now rumors arose that the prince was to wed the beautiful daughter of the neighboring king, and that it was for this reason he was having such a superb ship made ready to sail. The rumor ran that the prince's real interest in visiting the neighboring kingdom was to see the king's daughter and that he was to travel with a lordly retinue. The little mermaid shook her head and smiled, for she knew the prince's thoughts far better than anyone else did.

"I am forced to make this journey," he told her. "I must visit the beautiful princess, for this is my parents' wish, but they would not have me bring her home as my bride against my own will, and I can never love her. She does not resemble the lovely maiden in the temple, as you do, and if I were to choose a bride, I would sooner choose you, my dear mute foundling, with those telling eyes of yours." And he kissed her on the mouth, fingered her long hair, and laid his head against her heart so that she came to dream of mortal happiness and an immortal soul.

"I trust you aren't afraid of the sea, my silent child," he said, as they went on board the magnificent vessel that was to carry them to the land of the neighboring king. And he told her stories of storms, of ships becalmed, of strange deep-sea fish, and of the wonders that divers have seen. She smiled at such stories, for no one knew about the bottom of the sea as well as she did.

In the clear moonlight, when everyone except the man at the helm was asleep, she sat on the side of the ship gazing down through the transparent water, and fancied she could catch glimpses of her father's palace. On the topmost tower stood her old grandmother, wearing her silver crown and looking up at the keel of the ship through the rushing waves. Then her sisters rose to the surface, looking at her sadly, and wrung their white hands. She smiled and waved, trying to let them know that all went well and that she was happy. But along came the cabin boy, and her sisters dived out of sight so quickly that the boy supposed the flash of white he had seen was merely foam on the sea.

Next morning the ship came in to the harbor of the neighboring king's glorious city. All the church bells chimed, and trumpets were sounded from all the high towers, while the soldiers lined up with flying banners and glittering bayonets. Every day had a new festivity, as one ball or levee followed another, but the princess was still to appear. They said she was being brought up in some faraway sacred temple, where she

*She looked once more at the prince,
hurled herself over the bulwarks into the sea,
and felt her body dissolve in foam.*

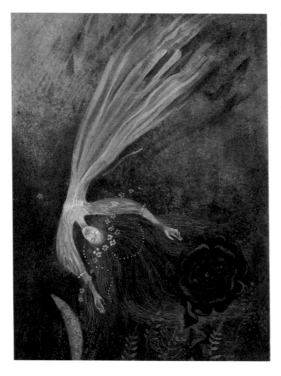

was learning every royal virtue. But she came at last.

The little mermaid was curious to see how beautiful this princess was, and she had to grant that a more exquisite figure she had never seen. The princess's skin was clear and fair, and behind the long, dark lashes her deep blue eyes were smiling and devoted.

"It was you!" the prince cried. "You are the one who saved me when I lay like a dead man beside the sea." He clasped the blushing bride of his choice in his arms. "Oh, I am happier than a man should be!" he told his little mermaid. "My fondest dream—that which I never dared to hope—has come true. You will share in my great joy, for you love me more than anyone does."

The little mermaid kissed his hand and felt that her heart was beginning to break. For the morning after his wedding day would see her dead and turned into watery foam.

All the church bells rang out, and heralds rode through the streets to announce the wedding. Upon every altar sweet-scented oils were burned in costly silver lamps. The priests swung their censers, the bride and the bridegroom joined their hands, and the bishop blessed their marriage. The little mermaid, clothed in silk and cloth of gold, held the bride's train, but she was deaf to the wedding march and blind to the holy ritual. Her thoughts turned on her last night upon earth, and on all she had lost in this world.

That same evening, the bride and bridegroom went aboard the ship. Cannon thundered and banners waved. On the deck of the ship a royal pavilion of purple and gold was set up, and furnished with luxurious cushions. Here the wedded couple were to sleep on that calm, clear night. The sails swelled in the breeze, and the ship glided so lightly that it scarcely seemed to move over the quiet sea. All nightfall brightly colored lanterns were lighted, and the mariners merrily danced on the deck. The little mermaid could not forget that first time she rose from the depths of the sea and looked on at such pomp and happiness. Light as a swallow pursued by his enemies, she joined in the whirling dance. Everyone cheered her, for never had she danced so wonderfully. Her tender feet felt as if they were pierced by daggers, but she did not feel it. Her heart suffered far greater pain. She knew that this was the last evening that she would see him for whom she had forsaken her home and family, for whom she had sacrificed her lovely voice and suffered such constant torment, while he knew nothing of all these things. It was the last night that she would breathe the same air with him, or look upon deep waters or the star fields of the blue sky. A never-ending night, without thought and without dreams, awaited her who had no soul and could not get one. The merrymaking lasted long after midnight, yet she laughed and danced on, despite the thought of death she carried in her heart. The prince kissed his beautiful bride and she toyed with his coal-black hair. Hand in hand, they went to rest in the magnificent pavilion.

A hush came over the ship. Only the helmsman remained on deck as the little mermaid leaned her white arms on the bulwarks and looked to

the east to see the first red hint of daybreak, for she knew that the first
flash of the sun would strike her dead. Then she saw her sisters rise up
among the waves. They were as pale as she, and there was no sign of
their lovely long hair that the breezes used to blow. It had all been cut off.
"We have given our hair to the witch," they said, "so that she would
send you help, and save you from death tonight. She gave us a knife. Here
it is. See the sharp blade! Before the sun rises, you must strike it into
the prince's heart, and when his warm blood bathes your feet they will
grow together and become a fish tail. Then you will be a mermaid again,
able to come back to us in the sea, and live out your three hundred years
before you die and turn into dead salt-sea foam. Make haste! He or you
must die before sunrise. Our old grandmother is so grief-stricken that her
white hair is falling fast, just as ours did under the witch's scissors. Kill
the prince and come back to us. Hurry! Hurry! See that red glow in the
heavens! In a few minutes the sun will rise and you must die." So saying,
they gave a strange deep sigh and sank beneath the waves.

The little mermaid parted the purple curtains of the tent and saw the
beautiful bride asleep with her head on the prince's breast. The mermaid
bent down and kissed his shapely forehead. She looked at the sky, fast
reddening for the break of day. She looked at the sharp knife and again
turned her eyes toward the prince, who in his sleep murmured the name
of his bride. His thoughts were all for her, and the knife blade trembled
in the mermaid's hand. But then she flung it from her, far out over the
waves. Where it fell the waves were red, as if bubbles of blood seethed in
the water. With eyes already glazing she looked once more at the prince,
hurled herself over the bulwarks into the sea, and felt her body dissolve
in foam.

The sun rose up from the waters. Its beams fell, warm and kindly,
upon the chill sea foam, and the little mermaid did not feel the hand
of death. In the bright sunlight overhead, she saw hundreds of fair

ethereal beings. They were so transparent that through them she could see the ship's white sails and the red clouds in the sky. Their voices were sheer music, but so spiritlike that no human ear could detect the sound, just as no eye on earth could see their forms. Without wings, they floated as light as the air itself. The little mermaid discovered that she was shaped like them, and that she was gradually rising up out of the foam.

"Who are you, toward whom I rise?" she asked, and her voice sounded like those above her, so spiritual that no music on earth could match it.

"We are the daughters of the air," they answered. "A mermaid has no immortal soul, and can never get one unless she wins the love of a human being. Her eternal life must depend on a power outside herself. The daughters of the air do not have an immortal soul either, but they can earn one by their good deeds. We fly to the south, where the hot poisonous air kills human beings unless we bring cool breezes. We carry the scent of flowers through the air, bringing freshness and healing balm wherever we go. When for three hundred years we have tried to do all the good that we can, we are given an immortal soul and a share in mankind's eternal bliss. You, poor little mermaid, have tried with your whole heart to do this, too. Your suffering and your loyalty have raised you up into the realm of airy spirits, and now in the course of three hundred years you may earn by your good deeds a soul that will never die."

The little mermaid lifted her clear bright eyes toward God's sun, and for the first time her eyes were wet with tears.

On board the ship all was astir and lively again. She saw the prince and his fair bride in search of her. Then they gazed sadly into the seething foam, as if they knew she had hurled herself into the waves. Unseen by them, she kissed the bride's forehead, smiled upon the prince, and rose up with the other daughters of the air to the rose-red clouds that sailed on high.

Sunbeams fell and the little mermaid
did not feel the hand of death.
In the sunlight overhead,
she saw hundreds of fair ethereal beings.

"This is the way that we shall rise to the kingdom of God, after three hundred years have passed."

"We may get there even sooner," one spirit whispered. "Unseen, we fly into the homes of men, where there are children, and for every day on which we find a good child who pleases his parents and deserves their love, God shortens our days of trial. The child does not know when we float through his rooms, but when we smile at him in approval one year is taken from our three hundred. But if we see a naughty, mischievous child we must shed tears of sorrow, and each tear adds a day to the time of our trial."

The Emperor's New Clothes

In 1837, the same exciting year he published "The Little Mermaid," Andersen released his famous satire about an emperor fooled by con artists into wearing invisible clothes. Like in "The Swineherd," Andersen chides the vanity and hypocrisy of inept royalty. Beloved around the world, the tale is loosely based on a story about a Moorish king that appeared in medieval Spain. Some historians claim that the theme dates to the second century AD. The tale wittily decries the pomp and circumstance of an ostentatious royal and his sycophantic advisors. But there is more: Just as Andersen's new book of tales was about to be printed, he added a new ending in which a young child decries the emperor's nakedness. Knowing nothing of the swindle, the child reveals the tricksters' escapades and the emperor's folly. With this new ending, three generations come into play: The elder emperor has power and status; the swindling men have cunning; but the child speaks the truth. No matter what tricks are employed, or how tightly power is gripped, the youngest generation will prevail every time. The ending is a classic example of Andersen's belief that children are closest to the truth. —ND

Illustrations by Harry Clarke, Irish, 1916

The minister couldn't see anything, because there was nothing to see.
"Heaven have mercy," he thought. "Can it be that I'm a fool?"

any years ago there was an emperor so exceedingly fond of new clothes that he spent all his money on being well dressed. He cared nothing about reviewing his soldiers, going to the theater, or going for a ride in his carriage, except to show off his new clothes. He had a coat for every hour of the day, and instead of saying, as one might, about any other ruler, "The king's in council," here they always said, "The emperor's in his dressing room."

In the great city where he lived, life was always gay. Every day many strangers came to town, and among them one day came two swindlers. They let it be known they were weavers, and they said they could weave the most magnificent fabrics imaginable. Not only were their colors and patterns uncommonly fine, but clothes made of this cloth had a wonderful way of becoming invisible to anyone who was unfit for his office, or who was unusually stupid.

"Those would be just the clothes for me," thought the emperor. "If I wore them I would be able to discover which men in my empire are unfit for their posts. And I could tell the wise men from the fools. Yes, I certainly must get some of the stuff woven for me right away." He paid the two swindlers a large sum of money to start work at once.

They set up two looms and pretended to weave, though there was nothing on the looms. All the finest silk and the purest gold thread, which they demanded, went into their traveling bags, while they worked the empty looms far into the night.

"I'd like to know how those weavers are getting on with the cloth," the emperor thought, but he felt slightly uncomfortable when he remembered that those who were unfit for their position would not be able to see the fabric. It couldn't have been that he doubted himself, yet he thought he'd rather send someone else to see how things were going. The whole town

"Isn't it a beautiful piece of goods?"
the swindlers asked the second official, as they displayed
and described their imaginary pattern.

knew about the cloth's peculiar power, and all were impatient to find out how stupid their neighbors were.

"I'll send my honest old minister to the weavers," the emperor decided. "He'll be the best one to tell me how the material looks, for he's a sensible man and no one does his duty better."

So the honest old minister went to the room where the two swindlers sat working away at their empty looms.

"Heaven help me," he thought as his eyes flew wide open. "I can't see anything at all." But he did not say so.

Both the swindlers begged him to be so kind as to come near to approve the excellent pattern, the beautiful colors. They pointed to the empty looms, and the poor old minister stared as hard as he dared. He couldn't see anything, because there was nothing to see. "Heaven have mercy," he thought. "Can it be that I'm a fool? I'd have never guessed it, and not a soul must know. Am I unfit to be the minister? It would never do to let on that I can't see the cloth."

"Don't hesitate to tell us what you think of it," said one of the weavers.

"Oh, it's beautiful—it's enchanting." The old minister peered through his spectacles. "Such a pattern, what colors! I'll be sure to tell the emperor how delighted I am with it."

"We're pleased to hear that," the swindlers said. They proceeded to name all the colors and to explain the intricate pattern. The old minister paid the closest attention, so that he could tell it all to the emperor. And so he did.

The swindlers at once asked for more money, more silk and gold thread, to get on with the weaving. But it all went into their pockets. Not a thread went into the looms, though they worked at their weaving as hard as ever.

The emperor presently sent another trustworthy official to see how the work progressed and how soon it would be ready. The same thing happened to him that had happened to the minister. He looked and he looked, but as there was nothing to see in the looms he couldn't see anything.

"Isn't it a beautiful piece of goods?" the swindlers asked him, as they displayed and described their imaginary pattern.

"I know I'm not stupid," the man thought, "so it must be that I'm unworthy of my good office. That's strange. I mustn't let anyone find it out, though." So he praised the material he did not see. He declared he was delighted with the beautiful colors and the exquisite pattern. To the emperor he said, "It held me spellbound."

All the town was talking of this splendid cloth, and the emperor wanted to see it for himself while it was still in the looms. Attended by a band of

"How well Your Majesty's new clothes look."
He heard on all sides, "That pattern, so perfect!
Those colors, so suitable! It is a magnificent outfit."

chosen men, among whom were his two old trusted officials—the ones who had been to the weavers—he set out to see the two swindlers. He found them weaving with might and main, but without a thread in their looms.

"Magnificent," said the two officials already duped. "Just look, Your Majesty, what colors! What a design!" They pointed to the empty looms, each supposing that the others could see the stuff.

"What's this?" thought the emperor. "I can't see anything. This is terrible! Am I a fool? Am I unfit to be the emperor? What a thing to happen to me of all people! Oh! It's *very* pretty," he said. "It has my highest approval." And he nodded approbation at the empty loom. Nothing could make him say that he couldn't see anything.

His whole retinue stared and stared. One saw no more than another, but they all joined the emperor in exclaiming, "Oh! It's *very* pretty," and they advised him to wear clothes made of this wonderful cloth especially for the great procession he was soon to lead. "Magnificent! Excellent! Unsurpassed!" were bandied from mouth to mouth, and everyone did his best to seem well pleased. The emperor gave each of the swindlers a cross to wear in his buttonhole, and the title of "Sir Weaver."

Before the procession the swindlers sat up all night and burned more than sixteen candles, to show how busy they were finishing the emperor's new clothes. They pretended to take the cloth off the loom. They made cuts in the air with huge scissors. And at last they said, "Now the emperor's new clothes are ready for him."

Then the emperor himself came with his noblest noblemen, and the swindlers each raised an arm as if they were holding something. They said, "These are the trousers, here's the coat, and this is the mantle," naming each garment. "All of them are as light as a spiderweb. One would almost think he had nothing on, but that's what makes them so fine."

"Exactly," all the noblemen agreed, though they could see nothing, for there was nothing to see.

"If Your Imperial Majesty will condescend to take your clothes off," said the swindlers, "we will help you on with your new ones here in front of the long mirror."

The emperor undressed, and the swindlers pretended to put his new clothes on him, one garment after another. They took him around the waist and seemed to be fastening something—that was his train—as the emperor turned round and round before the looking glass.

"How well Your Majesty's new clothes look. Aren't they becoming!" He heard on all sides, "That pattern, so perfect! Those colors, so suitable! It is a magnificent outfit."

Then the minister of public processions announced: "Your Majesty's canopy is waiting outside."

"Well, I'm supposed to be ready," the emperor said, and turned again for one last look in the mirror. "It is a remarkable fit, isn't it?" He seemed to regard his costume with the greatest interest.

The noblemen who were to carry his train stooped low and reached for the floor as if they were picking up his mantle. Then they pretended to lift and hold it high. They didn't dare admit they had nothing to hold.

So off went the emperor in procession under his splendid canopy. Everyone in the streets and the windows said, "Oh, how fine are the emperor's new clothes! Don't they fit him to perfection? And see his long train!" Nobody would confess that he couldn't see anything, for that would prove him either unfit for his position, or a fool. No costume the emperor had worn before was ever such a complete success.

"But he hasn't got anything on," a little child said.

"Did you ever hear such innocent prattle?" said its father. And one person whispered to another what the child had said, "He hasn't anything on. A child says he hasn't anything on."

"But he hasn't got anything on!" the whole town cried out at last.

The emperor shivered, for he suspected they were right. But he thought, "This procession has got to go on." So he walked more proudly than ever, as his noblemen held high the train that wasn't there at all.

The Steadfast
Tin Soldier

In 1838 Andersen wrote this touching story about a tin soldier whose pining love for a paper ballerina sustains him during a series of tumultuous misadventures. It features two motifs dear to Andersen—love and ballet—and he wrote the tale amidst an extraordinary change taking place in the dance world. Male dancers, who for centuries had dominated ballet, were being replaced by ballerinas as the stars. The watershed moment was Marie Taglioni's wildly popular performance in *La Sylphide* (*The Sylph*) in Paris in 1832. This new kind of ballerina, on her toes and in tulle, was electrifying—"a poetic vision of the ethereal," writes ballet historian Jennifer Homans. Andersen, who had originally wanted to be an actor and ballet dancer, was enchanted and used the image in many of his paper cuts, as on page 19. In the tale's tragic finale, he describes his airy protagonist as "a sylph," conjuring the popular supernatural beings. Ballets and fairy tales from this Romantic era shared other affinities, too: ill-fated love, all-consuming passion, spiritual ideals restrained by social expectations. Andersen paired the ballerina with a one-legged toy soldier who symbolized unflinching service and the aching vulnerabilities of a soldier's postwar life.—ND

Watercolor with ink illustrations by Kay Nielsen, Danish, 1924

here were once five-and-twenty tin soldiers. They were all brothers, born of the same old tin spoon. They shouldered their muskets and looked straight ahead of them, splendid in their uniforms, all red and blue.

The very first thing in the world that they heard was, "Tin soldiers!" A small boy shouted it and clapped his hands as the lid was lifted off their box on his birthday. He immediately set them up on the table.

All the soldiers looked exactly alike except one. He looked a little different as he had been cast last of all. The tin was short, so he had only one leg. But there he stood, as steady on one leg as any of the other soldiers on their two. But just you see, he'll be the remarkable one.

On the table with the soldiers were many other playthings, and one that no eye could miss was a marvelous castle of cardboard. It had little windows through which you could look right inside it. And in front of the castle were miniature trees around a little mirror supposed to represent a lake. The wax swans that swam on its surface were reflected in the mirror. All this was very pretty but prettiest of all was the little lady who stood in the open doorway of the castle. Though she was a paper doll, she wore a dress of the fluffiest gauze. A tiny blue ribbon went over her shoulder for a scarf, and in the middle of it shone a spangle that was as big as her face. The little lady held out both her arms, as a ballet dancer does, and one leg was lifted so high behind her that the tin soldier couldn't see it at all, and he supposed she must have only one leg, as he did.

"That would be a wife for me," he thought. "But maybe she's too grand. She lives in a castle. I have only a box, with four-and-twenty roommates to share it. That's no place for her. But I must try to make her acquaintance." Still as stiff as when he stood at attention, he lay down on the table behind a snuffbox, where he could admire the dainty little dancer

*Then the clock struck twelve and—clack!—
up popped the lid of the snuffbox.
Out bounced a little black bogey, a jack-in-the-box.*

who kept standing on one leg without ever losing her balance.

When the evening came the other tin soldiers were put away in their box, and the people of the house went to bed. Now the toys began to play among themselves at visits, and battles, and at giving balls. The tin soldiers rattled about in their box, for they wanted to play too, but they could not get the lid open. The nutcracker turned somersaults, and the slate pencil squeaked out jokes on the slate. The toys made such a noise that they woke up the canary bird, who gave them a speech, all in verse. The only two who stayed still were the tin soldier and the little dancer. Without ever swerving from the top of one toe, she held out her arms to him, and the tin soldier was just as steadfast on his one leg. Not once did he take his eyes off her.

Then the clock struck twelve and—*clack!*—up popped the lid of the snuffbox. But there was no snuff in it, no—out bounced a little black bogey, a jack-in-the-box.

"Tin soldier," he said. "Will you please keep your eyes to yourself?"

The tin soldier pretended not to hear.

The bogey said, "Just you wait till tomorrow."

But when morning came, and the children got up, the soldier was set on the window ledge. And whether the bogey did it, or there was a gust of wind, all of a sudden the window flew open and the soldier pitched out headlong from the third floor. He fell at breathtaking speed and landed cap first, with his bayonet buried between the paving stones and his one leg stuck straight in the air. The housemaid and the little boy ran down to look for him and, though they nearly stepped on the tin soldier, they walked right past without seeing him. If the soldier had called, "Here I am!" they would surely have found him, but he thought it contemptible to raise an uproar while he was wearing his uniform.

Soon it began to rain. The drops fell faster and faster, until they came down by the bucketful. As soon as the rain let up, along came two young rapscallions.

"Hi, look!" one of them said. "There's a tin soldier. Let's send him sailing."

They made a boat out of newspaper, put the tin soldier in the middle of it, and away he went down the gutter with the two young rapscallions running beside him and clapping their hands. High heavens! How the waves splashed, and how fast the water ran down the gutter. Don't forget that it had just been raining by the bucketful. The paper boat pitched, and tossed, and sometimes it whirled about so rapidly that it made the soldier's head spin. But he stood as steady as ever. Never once flinching, he kept his eyes front, and carried his gun shoulder-high. Suddenly the boat rushed under a long plank where the gutter was boarded over. It was as dark as the soldier's own box.

"Where can I be going?" the soldier wondered. "This must be that black bogey's revenge. Ah! If only I had the little lady with me, it could be twice as dark here for all that I would care."

Out popped a great water rat who lived under the gutter-plank.

"Have you a passport?" said the rat. "Hand it over."

The soldier kept quiet and held his musket tighter. On rushed the boat, and the rat came right after it, gnashing his teeth as he called to the sticks and straws:

"Halt him! Stop him! He didn't pay his toll. He hasn't shown his pass-port."

The paper boat broke beneath him,
and the soldier sank right through. Just then
he was swallowed by a most enormous fish.

But the current ran stronger and stronger. The soldier could see daylight ahead where the board ended, but he also heard a roar that would frighten the bravest of us. Hold on! Right at the end of that gutter-plank the water poured into the great canal. It was as dangerous to him as a waterfall would be to us.

He was so near it he could not possibly stop. The boat plunged into the whirlpool. The poor tin soldier stood as staunch as he could, and no one can say that he so much as blinked an eye. Thrice and again the boat spun around. It filled to the top and was bound to sink. The water was up to his neck and still the boat went down, deeper, deeper, deeper, and the paper got soft and limp. Then the water rushed over his head. He thought of the pretty little dancer whom he'd never see again, and in his ears rang an old, old song:

"Farewell, farewell, O warrior brave,
Nobody can from Death thee save."

And now the paper boat broke beneath him, and the soldier sank right through. And just at that moment he was swallowed by a most enormous fish.

My! How dark it was inside that fish. It was darker than under the gutter-plank and it was so cramped, but the tin soldier still was staunch. He lay there full length, soldier fashion, with musket to his shoulder.

Then the fish flopped and floundered in a most unaccountable way. Finally it was perfectly still, and after a while something struck through him like a flash of lightning. The tin soldier saw daylight again, and he heard a voice say, "The tin soldier!" The fish

The door blew open. She flew like a sylph,
straight into the fire with the soldier,
blazed up in a flash, and was gone.

had been caught, carried to market, bought, and brought to a kitchen where the cook cut him open with her big knife.

She picked the soldier up bodily between her two fingers, and carried him off upstairs. Everyone wanted to see this remarkable traveler who had traveled about in a fish's stomach, but the tin soldier took no pride in it. They put him on the table and—lo and behold, what curious things can happen in this world—there he was, back in the same room as before. He saw the same children, the same toys were on the table, and there was the same fine castle with the pretty little dancer. She still balanced on one leg, with the other raised high. She too was steadfast. That touched the soldier so deeply that he would have cried tin tears, only soldiers never cry. He looked at her, and she looked at him, and never a word was said. Just as things were going so nicely for them, one of the little boys snatched up the tin soldier and threw him into the stove. He did it for no reason at all. That black bogey in the snuffbox must have put him up to it.

The tin soldier stood there dressed in flames. He felt a terrible heat, but whether it came from the flames or from his love he didn't know. He'd lost his splendid colors, maybe from his hard journey, maybe from grief, nobody can say.

He looked at the little lady, and she looked at him, and he felt himself melting. But still he stood steadfast, with his musket held trim on his shoulder.

Then the door blew open. A puff of wind struck the dancer. She flew like a sylph, straight into the fire with the soldier, blazed up in a flash, and was gone. The tin soldier melted, all in a lump. The next day, when a servant took up the ashes she found him in the shape of a little tin heart. But of the pretty dancer nothing was left except her spangle, and that was burned as black as a coal.

The
Snow Queen

One of Andersen's longest stories, "The Snow Queen," from 1844, tells of a little girl, Gerda, on a mission to rescue her best friend, the little boy Kay, from the Snow Queen. Divided into seven parts, the tale stars colorful characters that evoke the wild, supernatural creatures in the oral folk tales Andersen heard as a child: the Devil and his goblins, a good witch, a robber girl, snowflake monsters, angels, and others. Andersen creates a snowy weather system to express a moral dilemma: In the Snow Queen's icy realm, hearts are frozen, social interaction is nil, family ties are broken—in short, love and self-awareness totally cease. Andersen seems to be asking the reader, how do we open ourselves to knowledge of the world without losing sight of who we are (remaining, as he puts it, "children at heart")? The tale begins with an ingenious story of how evil came into being: The Devil creates a magic mirror that makes the world ugly, and when it breaks, the splinters spread wickedness. Andersen's classic wit is sprinkled throughout the tale. Upon meeting the Snow Queen, a frightened Kay tries to pray, but "all he could remember was his multiplication tables."—ND

Two-color drawings by Katharine Beverley and Elizabeth Ellender,
nationalities unknown, 1929

*Then the mirror trembled with such violence
that it slipped from their hands and fell to the earth,
where it shattered into bits.*

First Story

Which Has to Do with a Mirror and Its Fragments

ow then! We will begin. When the story is done you shall know a great deal more than you do now.

He was a terribly bad hobgoblin, a goblin of the very wickedest sort, and, in fact, he was the Devil himself. One day the Devil was in a very good humor because he had just finished a mirror that had this very peculiar power: Everything good and beautiful that was reflected in it seemed to dwindle to almost nothing at all, while everything that was worthless and ugly became most conspicuous and even uglier than ever. In this mirror the loveliest landscapes looked like boiled spinach, and the very best people became hideous, or stood on their heads and had no stomachs. Their faces were distorted beyond any recognition, and if a person had a freckle it was sure to spread until it covered both nose and mouth.

"That's very funny!" said the Devil. If a good, pious thought passed through anyone's mind, it showed in the mirror as a carnal grin, and the Devil laughed aloud at his ingenious invention.

All those who went to the hobgoblin's school—for he had a school of his own—told everyone that a miracle had come to pass. Now, they asserted, for the very first time you could see how the world and all its people really looked. They scurried about with the mirror until there was not a person alive nor a land on earth that had not been distorted.

Then they wanted to fly up to Heaven itself, to scoff at the angels, and our Lord. The higher they flew with the mirror, the wider it grinned. They could hardly manage to hold it. Higher they flew, and higher still, nearer to Heaven and the angels. Then the grinning mirror trembled with such violence that it slipped from their hands and fell to the earth, where it shattered into hundreds of millions of billions of bits, or perhaps even more. And now it caused more trouble than it did before it was broken,

because some of the fragments were smaller than a grain of sand and these went flying throughout the wide world. Once they got in people's eyes they would stay there. These bits of glass distorted everything the people saw, and made them see only the bad side of things, for every little bit of glass kept the same power that the whole mirror had possessed.

A few people even got a glass splinter in their hearts, and that was a terrible thing, for it turned their hearts into lumps of ice. Some of the fragments were so large that they were used as windowpanes—but not the kind of window through which you should look at your friends. Other pieces were made into spectacles, and evil things came to pass when people put them on to see clearly and to see justice done. The fiend was so tickled by it all that he laughed till his sides were sore. But fine bits of the glass are still flying through the air, and now you shall hear what happened.

Second Story
A Little Boy and a Little Girl

In the big city it was so crowded with houses and people that few found room for even a small garden and most people had to be content with a flowerpot, but two poor children who lived there managed to have a garden that was a little bigger than a flowerpot. These children were not brother and sister, but they loved each other just as much as if they had been. Their parents lived close to one another in the garrets of two adjoining houses. Where the roofs met and where the rain gutter ran between the two houses, their two small windows faced each other. One had only to step across the rain gutter to go from window to window.

In these windows, the parents had a large box where they planted vegetables for their use, and a little rosebush, too. Each box had a bush that thrived to perfection. Then it occurred to the parents to put these boxes across the gutter, where they very nearly reached from one window to the other, and looked exactly like two walls of flowers. The pea plants hung down

*The rosebushes threw out long sprays that framed
the windows and bent over toward each other.
It was like a triumphal arch of greenery and flowers.*

over the boxes, and the rosebushes threw out long sprays that framed the windows and bent over toward each other. It was almost like a little triumphal arch of greenery and flowers. The boxes were very high, and the children knew that they were not to climb about on them, but they were often allowed to take their little stools out on the roof under the roses, where they had a wonderful time playing together.

Winter, of course, put an end to this pleasure. The windows often frosted over completely. But they would heat copper pennies on the stove and press these hot coins against the frost-coated glass. Then they had the finest of peepholes, as round as a ring, and behind them appeared a bright, friendly eye, one at each window—it was the little boy and the little girl who peeped out. His name was Kay and hers was Gerda. With one skip they could join each other in summer, but to visit together in the wintertime they had to go all the way downstairs in one house, and climb all the way upstairs in the other. Outside the snow was whirling.

"See the white bees swarming," the old grandmother said.

"Do they have a queen bee, too?" the little boy asked, for he knew that real bees have one.

"Yes, indeed they do," the grandmother said. "She flies in the thick of the swarm. She is the biggest bee of all, and can never stay quietly on the

Kay and Gerda were looking at a picture book,
and it was then that Kay cried: "Oh! Something hurt my heart.
I've got something in my eye."

earth, but goes back again to the dark clouds. Many a wintry night she flies through the streets and peers in through the windows. Then they freeze over in a strange fashion, as if they were covered with flowers."

"Oh yes, we've seen that," both the children said, and so they knew it was true.

"Can the Snow Queen come in here?" the little girl asked.

"Well, let her come!" cried the boy. "I would put her on the hot stove and melt her."

But Grandmother stroked his head, and told them other stories.

That evening when little Kay was at home and half ready for bed, he climbed on the chair by the window and looked out through the little peephole. A few snowflakes were falling, and the largest flake of all alight-

ed on the edge of one of the flower boxes. This flake grew bigger and bigger, until at last it turned into a woman who was dressed in the finest white gauze, which looked as if it had been made from millions of star-shaped flakes. She was beautiful and she was graceful, but she was ice—shining, glittering ice. She was alive, for all that, and her eyes sparkled like two bright stars, but in them there was neither rest nor peace. She nodded toward the window and beckoned with her hand. The little boy was frightened, and as he jumped down from the chair it seemed to him that a huge bird flew past the window.

The next day was clear and cold. Then the snow thawed, and spring-time came. The sun shone, the green grass sprouted, swallows made their nests, windows were thrown open, and once again the children played in their little roof garden, high up in the rain gutter on top of the house.

That summer the roses bloomed their splendid best. The little girl had learned a hymn in which there was a line about roses that reminded her of their own flowers. She sang it to the little boy, and he sang it with her:

"Where roses bloom so sweetly in the vale,
There shall you find the Christ Child,
without fail."

The children held each other by the hand, kissed the roses, looked up at the Lord's clear sunshine, and spoke to it as if the Christ Child were there. What glorious summer days those were, and how beautiful it was out under those fragrant rosebushes, which seemed as if they would never stop blooming.

Kay and Gerda were looking at a picture book of birds and beasts one day, and it was then—just as the clock in the church tower was striking five—that Kay cried:

"Oh! Something hurt my heart. And now I've got something in my eye."

The little girl put her arm around his neck, and he blinked his eye. No, she couldn't see anything in it.

"I think it's gone," he said. But it was not gone. It was one of those splinters of glass from the magic mirror. You remember that goblin's mirror—the one that made everything great and good that was reflected in it appear small and ugly, but which magnified all evil things until each blemish loomed large. Poor Kay! A fragment had pierced his heart as well, and soon it would turn into a lump of ice. The pain had stopped, but the glass was still there.

"Why should you be crying?" he asked. "It makes you look so ugly. There's nothing the matter with me." And suddenly he took it into his head to say:

"Ugh! That rose is all worm-eaten. And look, this one is crooked. And these roses, they are just as ugly as they can be. They look like the boxes they grow in." He gave the boxes a kick, and broke off both of the roses.

"Kay! What are you doing?" the little girl cried. When he saw how it upset her, he broke off another rose and then leaped home through his own window, leaving dear little Gerda all alone.

Afterwards, when she brought out her picture book, he said it was fit only for babes in the cradle. And whenever Grandmother told stories, he always broke in with a "but—." If he could manage it he would steal behind her, perch a pair of spectacles on his nose, and imitate her. He did this so cleverly that it made everybody laugh, and before long he could mimic the walk and the talk of everyone who lived on that street. Everything that was odd or ugly about them, Kay could mimic so well that people said, "That boy has surely got a good head on him!" But it was the glass in his eye and the glass in his heart that made him tease even little Gerda, who loved him with all her soul.

Now his games were very different from what they used to be. They became more sensible. When the snow was flying about one wintry day, he brought a large magnifying glass out of doors and spread the tail of his blue coat to let the snowflakes fall on it.

"Now look through the glass," he told Gerda. Each snowflake seemed much larger, and looked like a magnificent flower or a ten-pointed star. It was marvelous to look at.

"Look, how artistic!" said Kay. "They are much more interesting to look at than real flowers, for they are absolutely perfect. There isn't a flaw in them, until they start melting."

A little while later Kay came down with his big gloves on his hands and his sled on his back. Right in Gerda's ear he bawled out, "I've been given permission to play in the big square where the other boys are!" And away he ran.

"Now look through the magnifying glass," he told Gerda.
Each snowflake seemed much larger, and
looked like a magnificent flower or a ten-pointed star.

In the square some of the more adventuresome boys would tie their little sleds on behind the farmers' carts, to be pulled along for quite a distance. It was wonderful sport. While the fun was at its height, a big sleigh drove up. It was painted entirely white, and the driver wore a white, shaggy fur cloak and white, shaggy cap. As the sleigh drove twice around the square, Kay quickly hooked his little sled behind it, and down the street they went, faster and faster. The driver turned around in a friendly fashion and nodded to Kay, just as if they were old acquaintances. Every time Kay

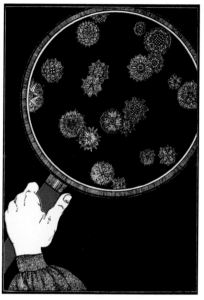

started to unfasten his little sled, its driver nodded again, and Kay held on, even when they drove right out through the town gate.

Then the snow began to fall so fast that the boy could not see his hands in front of him, as they sped on. He suddenly let go the slack of the rope in his hands, in order to get loose from the big sleigh, but it did no good. His little sled was tied on securely, and they went like the wind. He gave a loud shout, but nobody heard him. The snow whirled and the sleigh flew along. Every now and then it gave a jump, as if it were clearing hedges and ditches. The boy was terror-stricken. He tried to say his prayers, but all he could remember was his multiplication tables.

The snowflakes got bigger and bigger, until they looked like big white hens. All of a sudden the curtain of snow parted, and the big sleigh stopped and the driver stood up. The fur coat and the cap were made of

"Are you still cold?" the Snow Queen asked,
and kissed him on the forehead.
B-r-r-r! *That kiss was colder than ice.*

snow, and it was a woman, tall and slender and blinding white—she was the Snow Queen herself.

"We have made good time," she said. "Is it possible that you tremble from cold? Crawl under my bear coat." She took him up in the sleigh beside her, and as she wrapped the fur about him he felt as if he were sinking into a snowdrift.

"Are you still cold?" she asked, and kissed him on the forehead. *B-r-r-r!* That kiss was colder than ice. He felt it right down to his heart, half of which was already an icy lump. He felt as if he were dying, but only for a moment. Then he felt quite comfortable, and no longer noticed the cold.

"My sled! Don't forget my sled!" It was the only thing he thought of. They tied it to one of the white hens, which flew along after them with the sled on its back. The Snow Queen kissed Kay once more, and then he forgot little Gerda, and Grandmother, and all the others at home.

"You won't get any more kisses now," she said, "or else I should kiss you to death." Kay looked at her. She was so beautiful! A cleverer and prettier face he could not imagine. She no longer seemed to be made of ice, as she had seemed when she sat outside his window and beckoned to him. In his eyes she was perfect, and he was not at all afraid. He told her how he could do mental arithmetic even with fractions, and that he knew the size and population of all the countries. She kept on smiling, and he began to be afraid that he did not know as much as he thought he did. He looked up at the great big space overhead, as she flew with him high up on the black clouds, while the storm whistled and roared as if it were singing old ballads.

They flew over forests and lakes, over many a land and sea. Below them the wind blew cold, wolves howled, and black crows screamed as they skimmed across the glittering snow. But up above the moon shone bright and large, and on it Kay fixed his eyes throughout that long, long winter night. By day he slept at the feet of the Snow Queen.

They flew over many a land and sea.
The wind blew cold, wolves howled, and black crows screamed
as they skimmed across the snow.

Third Story
The Flower Garden of the
Woman Skilled in Magic

How did little Gerda get along when Kay did not come back? Where could he be? Nobody knew. Nobody could give them any news of him. All that the boys could say was that they had seen him hitch his little sled to a fine big sleigh, which had driven down the street and out through the town gate. Nobody knew what had become of Kay. Many tears were shed, and little Gerda sobbed hardest of all. People said that he was dead— that he must have been drowned in the river not far from town. Ah, how gloomy those long winter days were!

But spring and its warm sunshine came at last.

"Kay is dead and gone," little Gerda said.

"I don't believe it," said the sunshine.

"He's dead and gone," she said to the swallows.

"We don't believe it," they sang. Finally little Gerda began to disbelieve it, too. One morning she said to herself:

"I'll put on my new red shoes, the ones Kay has never seen, and I'll go down by the river to ask about him."

It was very early in the morning. She kissed her old grandmother, who was still asleep, put on her red shoes, and all by herself she hurried out through the town gate and down to the river.

"Is it true that you have taken my own little playmate? I'll give you my red shoes if you will bring him back to me."

It seemed to her that the waves nodded very strangely. So she took off the red shoes that were her dearest possession, and threw them into the river. But they fell near the shore, and the little waves washed them right back to her. It seemed that the river could not take her dearest possession, because it did not have little Kay. However, she was afraid that she had not thrown them far enough, so she clambered into a boat that lay among the reeds, walked to the end of it, and threw her shoes out into the water again. But the boat was not tied, and her movements made it drift away from the bank. She realized this, and tried to get ashore, but by the time she reached the other end of the boat it was already more than a yard from the bank, and was fast gaining speed.

Little Gerda was so frightened that she began to cry, and no one was there to hear her except the sparrows. They could not carry her to land, but they flew along the shore twittering, "We are here! Here we are!" as if to comfort her. The boat drifted swiftly down the stream, and Gerda sat there quite still, in her stocking feet. Her little red shoes floated along behind, but they could not catch up with her because the boat was gathering headway. It was very pretty on both sides of the river, where the flowers were lovely, the trees were old, and the hillsides afforded pasture for cattle and sheep. But not one single person did Gerda see.

"Perhaps the river will take me to little Kay," she thought, and that made her feel more cheerful. She stood up and watched the lovely green banks for hour after hour.

Then she came to a large cherry orchard, in which there was a little house with strange red and blue windows. It had a thatched roof, and outside it stood two wooden soldiers, who presented arms to everyone who sailed past.

Gerda thought they were alive, and called out to them, but of course they did not answer her. She drifted quite close to them as the current drove the boat toward the bank. Gerda called even louder, and an old, old woman came out of the house. She leaned on a crooked stick; she had on a big sun hat, and on it were painted the most glorious flowers.

"You poor little child!" the old woman exclaimed. "However did you get lost on this big swift river, and however did you drift so far into the great wide world?" The old woman waded right into the water, caught hold of the boat with her crooked stick, pulled it in to shore, and lifted little Gerda out of it.

Gerda was very glad to be on dry land again, but she felt a little afraid of this strange old woman, who said to her:

"Come and tell me who you are, and how you got here." Gerda told her all about it. The woman shook her head and said, "Hmm, hmm!" And when Gerda had told her everything and asked if she hadn't seen little Kay, the woman said he had not yet come by, but that he might be along any day now. And she told Gerda not to take it so to heart, but to taste her cherries and look at her flowers. These were more beautiful than any picture book, and each one had a story to tell. Then she led Gerda by the hand into her little house, and the old woman locked the door.

The windows were placed high up on the walls, and through their red, blue, and yellow panes the sunlight streamed in a strange mixture of all the colors there are. But on the table were the most delicious cherries, and Gerda, who was no longer afraid, ate as many as she liked. While she was eating them, the old woman combed her hair with a golden comb. Gerda's pretty hair fell in shining yellow ringlets on either side of a friendly little face that was as round and blooming as a rose.

"I've so often wished for a dear little girl like you," the old woman told her. "Now you'll see how well the two of us will get along." While her hair was being combed, Gerda gradually forgot all about Kay, for the old woman

An old, old woman came out of the house.
She leaned on a stick, and on her hat were painted glorious flowers.

was skilled in magic. But she was
not a wicked witch. She only dab-
bled in magic to amuse herself, but
she wanted very much to keep little
Gerda. So she went out into her garden and pointed her crooked stick at
all the rosebushes. In the full bloom
of their beauty, all of them sank
down into the black earth, without
leaving a single trace behind. The
old woman was afraid that if Gerda
saw them they would remind her so
strongly of her own roses, and of little Kay, that she would run away
again.

Then Gerda was led into the flower garden. How fragrant and lovely
it was! Every known flower of every
season was there in full bloom. No picture book was ever so pretty and gay.
Gerda jumped for joy, and played in the garden until the sun went down
behind the tall cherry trees. Then she was tucked into a beautiful bed, under a red silk coverlet quilted with blue violets. There she slept, and there
she dreamed as gloriously as any queen on her wedding day.

The next morning she again went out into the warm sunshine to play
with the flowers—and this she did for many a day. Gerda knew every
flower by heart, and, plentiful though they were, she always felt that there
was one missing, but which one she didn't quite know. One day she sat
looking at the old woman's sun hat, and the prettiest of all the flowers
painted on it was a rose. The old woman had forgotten this rose on her hat
when she made the real roses disappear in the earth. But that's just the

Gerda was led into the flower garden.
How fragrant and lovely it was!
Every known flower of every season was there in full bloom.

sort of thing that happens when one doesn't stop to think.

"Why aren't there any roses here?" said Gerda. She rushed out among the flower beds, and she looked and she looked, but there wasn't a rose to be seen. Then she sat down and cried. But her hot tears fell on the very spot where a rosebush had sunk into the ground, and when her warm tears moistened the earth the bush sprang up again, as full of blossoms as when it disappeared. Gerda hugged it, and kissed the roses. She remembered her own pretty roses, and thought of little Kay.

"Oh how long I have been delayed," the little girl said. "I should have been looking for Kay. Don't you know where he is?" she asked the roses. "Do you think that he is dead and gone?"

"He isn't dead," the roses told her. "We have been down in the earth where the dead people are, but Kay is not there."

"Thank you," said little Gerda, who went to all the other flowers, put her lips near them and asked, "Do you know where little Kay is?"

But every flower stood in the sun, and dreamed its own fairy tale, or its story. Though Gerda listened to many, many of them, not one of the flowers knew anything about Kay.

What did the tiger lily say?

"Do you hear the drum? *Boom, boom!* It has only two notes, always *boom, boom!* Hear the women wail. Hear the priests chant. The Hindu woman in her long red robe stands on the funeral pyre. The flames rise around her and her dead husband, but the Hindu woman is thinking of that living man in the crowd around them. She is thinking of him whose eyes are burning hotter than the flames—of him whose fiery glances have pierced her heart more deeply than these flames that soon will burn her body to ashes. Can the flame of the heart die in the flame of the funeral pyre?"

"I don't understand that at all," little Gerda said.

"That's my fairy tale," said the lily.

What did the trumpet flower say?

"An ancient castle rises high from a narrow path in the mountains. The thick ivy grows leaf upon leaf where it climbs to the balcony. There stands a beautiful maiden. She leans out over the balustrade to look down the path. No rose on its stem is as graceful as she, nor is any apple blossom in the breeze so light. Hear the rustle of her silken gown, sighing, 'Will he never come?'"

"Do you mean Kay?" little Gerda asked.

"I am talking about my story, my own dream," the trumpet flower replied.

What did the little snowdrop say?

"Between the trees a board hangs by two ropes. It is a swing. Two pretty little girls, with frocks as white as snow, and long green ribbons fluttering from their hats, are swinging. Their brother, who is bigger than they are, stands behind them on the swing, with his arms around the ropes to hold himself. In one hand he has a little cup, and in the other a clay pipe. He is blowing soap bubbles, and as the swing flies the bubbles float off in all their changing colors. The last bubble is still clinging to the bowl of his pipe, and fluttering in the air as the swing sweeps to and fro. High and low the swing flies, until the dog loses his balance, barks, and loses his temper. They tease him, and the bubble bursts. A swinging board pictured in a bubble before it broke—that is my story."

"It may be a very pretty story, but you told it very sadly and you didn't mention Kay at all."

What did the hyacinths say?

"There were three sisters, quite transparent and very fair. One wore a red dress, the second wore a blue one, and the third went all in white. Hand in hand they danced in the clear moonlight, beside a calm lake. They were not elfin folk. They were human beings. The air was sweet, and the sisters disappeared into the forest. The fragrance of the air grew sweeter. Three coffins, in which lie the three sisters, glide out of the forest and across the lake. The fireflies hover about them like little flickering lights. Are the dancing sisters sleeping or are they dead? The fragrance of the flowers says they are dead, and the evening bell tolls for their funeral."

"You are making me very unhappy," little Gerda said. "Your fragrance is so strong that I cannot help thinking of those dead sisters. Oh, could little Kay really be dead? The roses have been down under the ground, and they say no."

"Ding, dong," tolled the hyacinth bells. "We do not toll for little Kay. We do not know him. We are simply singing our song—the only song we know."

And Gerda went on to the buttercup that shone among its glossy green leaves.

"You are like a bright little sun," said Gerda. "Tell me, do you know where I can find my playmate?"

And the buttercup shone brightly as it looked up at Gerda. But what sort of song would a buttercup sing? It certainly wouldn't be about Kay.

"In a small courtyard, God's sun was shining brightly on the very first day of spring. Its beams glanced along the white wall of the house next door, and close by grew the first yellow flowers of spring shining like gold in the warm sunlight. An old grandmother was sitting outside in her chair. Her granddaughter, a poor but very pretty maidservant, had just come

*Gerda's hot tears fell on the very spot
where a rosebush had sunk into the ground,
and the bush sprang up again.*

home for a little visit. She kissed her grandmother, and there was gold, a heart full of gold, in that kiss. Gold on her lips, gold in her dreams, and gold above in the morning beams. There, I've told you my little story," said the buttercup.

"Oh, my poor old grandmother," said Gerda. "She will miss me so. She must be grieving for me as much as she did for little Kay. But I'll soon go home again, and I'll bring Kay with me. There's no use asking the flowers about him. They don't know anything except their own songs, and they haven't any news for me."

Then she tucked up her little skirts so that she could run away faster, but the narcissus tapped her against the leg as she was jumping over it. So she stopped and leaned over the tall flower.

"Perhaps you have something to tell me," she said.

What did the narcissus say?

"I can see myself! I can see myself! Oh, how sweet is my own fragrance! Up in the narrow garret there is a little dancer, half dressed. First she stands on one leg. Then she stands on both, and kicks her heels at the whole world. She is an illusion of the stage. She pours water from the teapot over a piece of cloth she is holding—it is her bodice. Cleanliness is such a virtue! Her white dress hangs from a hook. It too has been washed in the teapot, and dried on the roof. She puts it on, and ties a saffron scarf around her neck to make the

Hand in hand the three sisters danced
in the moonlight, beside a calm lake.
They were not elfin folk. They were human beings.

dress seem whiter. Point your toes! See how straight she balances on that single stem? I can see myself! I can see myself!"

"I'm not interested," said Gerda. "What a thing to tell me about!"

She ran to the end of the garden, and though the gate was fastened she worked the rusty latch till it gave way and the gate flew open. Little Gerda scampered out into the wide world in her bare feet. She looked back three times, but nobody came after her. At last she could run no further, and she sat down to rest on a big stone, and when she looked up she saw that summer had gone by, and it was late in the fall. She could never have guessed it inside the beautiful garden where the sun was always shining, and the flowers of every season were always in full bloom.

"Gracious! How long I've dallied," Gerda said. "Fall is already here. I can't rest any longer."

She got up to run on, but how footsore and tired she was! And how cold and bleak everything around her looked! The long leaves of the willow tree had turned quite yellow, and damp puffs of mist dropped from them like drops of water. One leaf after another fell to the ground. Only the blackthorn still bore fruit, and its fruit was so sour that it set your teeth on edge.

Oh, how dreary and gray the wide world looked.

Fourth Story
The Prince and the Princess

The next time that Gerda was forced to rest, a big crow came hopping across the snow in front of her. For a long time he had been watching her and cocking his head to one side, and now he said, "Caw, caw! Good caw day! Good caw day!" He could not say it any better, but he felt kindly inclined toward the little girl, and asked her where she was going in the great wide world, all alone. Gerda understood him when he said "alone," and she knew its meaning all too well. She told the crow the whole story of her life, and asked if he hadn't seen Kay. The crow gravely nodded his head and cawed, "Maybe I have, maybe I have!"

"What! Do you really think you have?" the little girl cried, and almost hugged the crow to death as she kissed him.

"Gently, gently!" said the crow. "I think that it may have been little Kay that I saw, but if it was, then he has forgotten you for the princess."

"Does he live with a princess?" Gerda asked.

"Yes. Listen!" said the crow. "But it is so hard for me to speak your language. If you understand crow talk, I can tell you much more easily."

"I don't know the language," said Gerda. "My grandmother knows it, just as well as she knows baby talk, and I do wish I had learned it."

"No matter," said the crow. "I'll tell you as well as I can, though that won't be any too good." And he told her all that he knew.

"In the kingdom where they are now, there is a princess who is uncommonly clever, and no wonder. She has read all the newspapers in the world and forgotten them again—that's how clever she is. Well, not long ago she was sitting on her throne. That's by no means as much fun as people suppose, so she fell to humming an old tune, and the refrain of it happened to run:

'Why, oh, why, shouldn't I get married?'

"'Why, that's an idea!' said she. And she made up her mind to marry as soon as she could find the sort of husband who could give a good answer when anyone spoke to him, instead of one of those fellows who merely stand around looking impressive, for that is so tiresome. She had the drums drubbed to call together all her ladies-in-waiting, and when they heard what she had in mind they were delighted.

"'Oh, we like that!' they said. 'We were just thinking the very same thing.'

"Believe me," said the crow, "every word I tell you is true. I have a tame ladylove who has the run of the palace, and I had the whole story straight from her." Of course his ladylove was also a crow, for birds of a feather will flock together.

The little dancer puts her white dress on.
Point your toes! See how straight she balances on that single stem?

"The newspapers immediately came out with a border of hearts and the initials of the princess, and you could read an announcement that any presentable young man might go to the palace and talk with her. The one who spoke best, and who seemed most at home in the palace, would be chosen by the princess as her husband.

"Yes, yes," said the crow, "believe me, that's as true as it is that here I sit. Men flocked to the palace, and there was much crowding and crushing, but on neither the first nor the second day was anyone chosen. Out in the street they were all glib talkers, but after they entered the palace gate where the guardsmen were stationed in their silver-braided uniforms, and after they climbed up the staircase lined with footmen in gold-embroidered linen, they arrived in the brilliantly lighted reception halls without a word to say. And when they stood in front of the princess on her throne, the best they could do was to echo the last word of her remarks, and she didn't care to hear it repeated.

"It was just as if everyone in the throne room had his stomach filled with snuff and had fallen asleep; for as soon as they were back in the streets there was no stopping their talk.

"The line of candidates extended all the way from the town gates to the palace. I saw them myself," said the crow. "They got hungry and they got thirsty, but from the palace they got nothing—not even a glass of lukewarm

"He had a knapsack on his back," the crow told her.
"That must have been his sled," said Gerda.
"He was carrying it when he went away."

water. To be sure, some of the clever candidates had brought sandwiches with them, but they did not share them with their neighbors. Each man thought, 'Just let him look hungry, then the princess won't take him!'"

"But Kay, little Kay," Gerda interrupted, "when did he come? Was he among those people?"

"Give me time, give me time! We are just coming to him. On the third day a little person, with neither horse nor carriage, strode boldly up to the palace. His eyes sparkled the way yours do, and he had handsome long hair, but his clothes were poor."

"Oh, that was Kay!" Gerda said, and clapped her hands in glee. "Now I've found him."

"He had a little knapsack on his back," the crow told her.

"No, that must have been his sled," said Gerda. "He was carrying it when he went away."

"Maybe so," the crow said. "I didn't look at it carefully. But my tame ladylove told me that when he went through the palace gates and saw the guardsmen in silver, and on the staircase the footmen in gold, he wasn't at all taken aback. He nodded and said to them:

"'It must be very tiresome to stand on the stairs. I'd rather go inside.'

"The halls were brilliantly lighted. Ministers of state and privy councilors were walking about barefoot, carrying golden trays in front of them. It was enough to make anyone feel solemn, and his boots creaked dreadfully, but he wasn't a bit afraid."

"That certainly must have been Kay," said Gerda. "I know he was wearing new boots. I heard them creaking in Grandmother's room."

"Oh, they creaked all right," said the crow. "But it was little enough he cared as he walked straight to the princess, who was sitting on a pearl as big as a spinning wheel. All the ladies-in-waiting with their attendants and their attendants' attendants, and all the lords-in-waiting with their gentlemen and their gentlemen's men, each of whom had his page with him, were standing there, and the nearer they stood to the door the more arrogant they looked. The gentlemen's men's pages, who always wore slippers, were almost too arrogant to look as they stood at the threshold."

"That must have been terrible!" little Gerda exclaimed. "And yet Kay won the princess?"

"If I weren't a crow, I would have married her myself, for all that I'm engaged to another. They say he spoke as well as I do when I speak my crow language. Or so my tame ladylove tells me. He was dashing and handsome, and he was not there to court the princess but to hear her wisdom. This he liked, and she liked him."

"Of course it was Kay," said Gerda. "He was so clever that he could do mental arithmetic even with fractions. Oh, please take me to the palace."

"That's easy enough to say," said the crow, "but how can we manage it? I'll talk it over with my tame ladylove, and she may be able to suggest something, but I must warn you that a little girl like you will never be admitted."

"Oh, yes I shall," said Gerda. "When Kay hears about me, he will come out to fetch me at once."

"Wait for me beside that stile," the crow said. He wagged his head and off he flew.

Darkness had set in when he got back.

"Caw, caw!" he said. "My ladylove sends you her best wishes, and here's a little loaf of bread for you. She found it in the kitchen, where they have all the bread they need, and you must be hungry. You simply can't get into the palace with those bare feet. The guardsmen in silver and the footmen in gold would never permit it. But don't you cry. We'll find a way. My ladylove knows of a little back staircase that leads up to the bedroom, and she knows where they keep the key to it."

Then they went into the garden and down the wide promenade where the leaves were falling one by one. When, one by one, the lights went out in

"It seems that someone is on the stairs behind us," said Gerda.
Things brushed past, and from their shadows seemed to be horses
with spindly legs and waving manes.

the palace, the crow led little Gerda to the back door, which stood ajar.

Oh, how her heart did beat with fear and longing. It was just as if she were about to do something wrong, yet she only wanted to make sure that this really was little Kay. Yes, truly it must be Kay, she thought, as she recalled his sparkling eyes and his long hair. She remembered exactly how he looked when he used to smile at her as they sat under the roses at home. Wouldn't he be glad to see her! Wouldn't he be interested in hearing how far she had come to find him, and how sad they had all been when he didn't come home. She was so frightened, yet so happy.

Now they were on the stairway. A little lamp was burning on a cupboard, and there stood the tame crow, cocking her head to look at Gerda, who made the curtsy that her grandmother had taught her.

"My fiancé has told me many charming things about you, dear young lady," she said. "Your biography, as one might say, is very touching. Kindly take the lamp and I shall lead the way. We shall keep straight ahead, where we aren't apt to run into anyone."

"It seems to me that someone is on the stairs behind us," said Gerda. Things brushed past, and from their shadows on the wall they seemed to be horses with spindly legs and waving manes. And there were shadows of huntsmen, ladies and gentlemen, on horseback.

"Ouch!" the old woman howled.
At just that moment her own little daughter, a wild
and reckless creature, had bitten her ear.

"Those are only dreams," said the tame crow. "They come to take the thoughts of their royal masters off to the chase. That's just as well, for it will give you a good opportunity to see them while they sleep. But I trust that, when you rise to high position and power, you will show a grateful heart."

"Tut tut! You've no need to say that," said the forest crow.

Now they entered the first room. It was hung with rose-colored satin, embroidered with flowers. The dream shadows were flitting by so fast that Gerda could not see the lords and ladies. Hall after magnificent hall quite bewildered her, until at last they reached the royal bedroom.

The ceiling of it was like the top of a huge palm tree, with leaves of glass, costly glass. In the middle of the room two beds hung from a massive stem of gold. Each of them looked like a lily. One bed was white, and there lay the princess. The other was red, and there Gerda hoped to find little Kay. She bent one of the scarlet petals and saw the nape of a little brown neck. Surely this must be Kay. She called his name aloud and held the lamp near him. The dreams on horseback pranced into the room again, as he awoke— and turned his head—and it was not little Kay at all.

The prince only resembled Kay about the neck, but he was young and handsome. The princess peeked out of her lily-white bed, and asked what had happened. Little Gerda cried and told them all about herself, and about all that the crows had done for her.

"Poor little thing," the prince and princess said. They praised the crows, and said they weren't the least bit angry with them, but not to do it again. Furthermore, they should have a reward.

"Would you rather fly about without any responsibilities," said the princess, "or would you care to be appointed court crows for life, with rights to all scraps from the kitchen?"

Both the crows bowed low and begged for the permanent office, for they thought of their future and said it was better to provide for their "old age," as they called it.

The prince got up, and let Gerda have his bed. It was the utmost he could do. She clasped his little hands and thought, "How nice the people and the birds are." She closed her eyes, fell peacefully asleep, and all the dreams came flying back again. They looked like angels, and they drew a little sled on which Kay sat. He nodded to her, but this was only in a dream, so it all disappeared when she woke up.

The next day she was dressed from her head to her heels in silk and in velvet, too. They asked her to stay at the palace and have a nice time there, but instead she begged them to let her have a little carriage, a little horse, and a pair of little boots, so that she could drive out into the wide world to find Kay.

They gave her a pair of boots, and also a muff. They dressed her as nicely as could be and, when she was ready to go, there at the gate stood a brand-new carriage of pure gold. On it the coat of arms of the prince and princess glistened like a star.

The coachman, the footman, and the postilions—for postilions there were—all wore golden crowns. The prince and the princess themselves helped her into the carriage, and wished her Godspeed. The forest crow, who was now a married man, accompanied her for the first three miles, and sat beside Gerda, for it upset him to ride backward. The other crow stood beside the gate and waved her wings. She did not accompany them

Then the wood pigeons said,
"Coo, coo. We have seen little Kay.
He sat in the Snow Queen's sleigh."

because she was suffering from a headache, brought on by eating too much in her new position. Inside, the carriage was lined with sugared cookies, and the seats were filled with fruits and gingerbread.

"Fare you well, fare you well," called the prince and princess. Little Gerda cried and the crow cried too, for the first few miles. Then the crow said goodbye, and that was the saddest leave-taking of all. He flew up into a tree and waved his big black wings as long as he could see the carriage, which flashed as brightly as the sun.

Fifth Story
The Little Robber Girl

The carriage rolled on into a dark forest. Like a blazing torch, it shone in the eyes of some robbers. They could not bear it.

"That's gold! That's gold!" they cried. They sprang forward, seized the horses, killed the little postilions, the coachman, and the footman, and dragged little Gerda out of the carriage.

"How plump and tender she looks, just as if she'd been fattened on nuts!" cried the old robber woman, who had a long bristly beard, and long eyebrows that hung down over her eyes. "She looks like a fat little lamb. What a dainty dish she will be!" As she said this she drew out her knife, a dreadful, flashing thing.

"Ouch!" the old woman howled. At just that moment her own little daughter had bitten her ear. This little girl, whom she carried on her back, was a wild and reckless creature. "You beastly brat!" her mother exclaimed, but it kept her from using that knife on Gerda.

"She shall play with me," said the little robber girl. "She must give me her muff and that pretty dress she wears, and sleep with me in my bed." And she again gave her mother such a bite that the woman hopped and whirled around in pain. All of the robbers laughed, and shouted:

"See how she dances with her brat."

"I want to ride in the carriage," the little robber girl said, and ride she did, for she was too spoiled and headstrong for words. She and Gerda climbed into the carriage and away they drove over stumps and stones, into the depths of the forest. The little robber girl was no taller than Gerda, but she was stronger and much broader in the shoulders. Her skin was brown and her eyes coal-black—almost sad in their expression. She put her arm around Gerda, and said:

"They shan't kill you unless I get angry with you. I think you must be a princess."

"No, I'm not," said little Gerda. And she told about all that had happened to her, and how much she cared for little Kay. The robber girl looked at her gravely, gave a little nod of approval, and told her:

"Even if I should get angry with you, they shan't kill you, because I'll do it myself!" Then she dried Gerda's eyes, and stuck her own hands into Gerda's soft, warm muff.

The carriage stopped at last, in the courtyard of a robber's castle. The walls of it were cracked from bottom to top. Crows and ravens flew out of every loophole, and bulldogs huge enough to devour a man jumped high in the air. But they did not bark, for that was forbidden.

In the middle of the stone-paved, smoky old hall, a big fire was burning. The smoke of it drifted up to the ceiling, where it had to find its own way out. Soup was boiling in a big cauldron, and hares and rabbits were roasting on the spit.

"Tonight you shall sleep with me and all my little animals," the robber girl said. After they had something to eat and drink, they went over to a corner that was strewn with rugs and straw. On sticks and perches around the bedding roosted nearly a hundred pigeons. They seemed to be asleep, but they stirred just a little when the two girls came near them.

"They are all mine," said the little robber girl. She seized the one that was nearest to her, held it by the legs, and shook it until it flapped its wings.

"You must carry this little girl to the Snow Queen's palace,
where her playmate is," said the robber girl.
The reindeer was so happy he bounded into the air.

"Kiss it," she cried, and thrust the bird in Gerda's face. "Those two are the wild rascals," she said, pointing high up the wall to a hole barred with wooden sticks. "Rascals of the woods they are, and they would fly away in a minute if they were not locked up."

"And here is my old sweetheart, Bae," she said, pulling at the horns of a reindeer that was tethered by a shiny copper ring around his neck. "We have to keep a sharp eye on him, or he would run away from us, too. Every single night I tickle his neck with my knife blade, for he is afraid of that." From a hole in the wall she pulled a long knife and rubbed it against the reindeer's neck. After the poor animal had kicked up its heels, the robber girl laughed and pulled Gerda down into the bed with her.

"Are you going to keep that knife in bed with you?" Gerda asked, and looked at it a little frightened.

"I always sleep with my knife," the little robber girl said. "You never can tell what may happen. But let's hear again what you told me about little Kay, and why you are wandering through the wide world."

Gerda told the story all over again, while the wild pigeons cooed in their cage overhead, and the tame pigeons slept. The little robber girl clasped one arm around Gerda's neck, gripped her knife in the other hand, fell asleep, and snored so that one could hear her. But Gerda could not close her eyes at all. She did not know whether she was to live or whether she

"Those are my old northern lights," said the reindeer.
"See how they flash." On he ran, faster than ever, by night and day.

was to die. The robbers sat around their fire, singing and drinking, and the old robber woman was turning somersaults. It was a terrible sight for a little girl to see.

Then the wood pigeons said, "Coo, coo. We have seen little Kay. A white hen was carrying his sled, and Kay sat in the Snow Queen's sleigh. They swooped low, over the trees where we lay in our nest. The Snow Queen blew upon us, and all the young pigeons died except us. Coo, coo."

"What is that you are saying up there?" cried Gerda. "Where was the Snow Queen going? Do you know anything about it?"

"She was probably bound for Lapland, where they always have snow and ice. Why don't you ask the reindeer who is tethered beside you?"

"Yes, there is ice and snow in that glorious land," the reindeer told her. "You can prance about freely across those great, glittering fields. The Snow Queen has her summer tent there, but her stronghold is a castle up nearer the North Pole, on the island called Spitsbergen."

"Oh, Kay, little Kay," Gerda sighed.

"Lie still," said the little robber girl, "or I'll stick my knife in your stomach."

In the morning Gerda told her all that the wood pigeons had said. The little robber girl looked quite thoughtful. She nodded her head, and exclaimed, "Leave it to me! Leave it to me."

"Do you know where Lapland is?" she asked the reindeer.

"Who knows better than I?" the reindeer said, and his eyes sparkled. "There I was born, there I was bred, and there I kicked my heels in freedom, across the fields of snow."

"Listen!" the robber girl said to Gerda. "As you see, all the men are away. Mother is still here, and here she'll stay, but before the morning is over she will drink out of that big bottle, and then she usually dozes off for a nap. As soon as that happens, I will do you a good turn."

She jumped out of bed, rushed over and threw her arms around her mother's neck, pulled at her beard bristles, and said, "Good morning, my dear nanny goat." Her mother thumped her nose until it was red and blue, but all that was done out of pure love.

As soon as the mother had tipped up the bottle and dozed off to sleep, the little robber girl ran to the reindeer and said, "I have a good notion to keep you here, and tickle you with my sharp knife. You are so funny when I do, but never mind that. I'll untie your rope, and help you find your way outside, so that you can run back to Lapland. But you must put your best leg forward and carry this little girl to the Snow Queen's palace, where her playmate is. I suppose you heard what she told me, for she spoke so loud, and you were eavesdropping."

The reindeer was so happy that he bounded into the air. The robber girl hoisted little Gerda on his back, carefully tied her in place, and even gave her a little pillow to sit on. "I don't do things halfway," she said. "Here, take back your fur boots, for it's going to be bitter cold. I'll keep your muff, because it's such a pretty one. But your fingers mustn't get cold. Here are my mother's big mittens, which will come right up to your elbows. Pull them on. Now your hands look just like my ugly mother's big paws."

And Gerda shed happy tears.

"I don't care to see you blubbering," said the little robber girl. "You ought to be pleased now. Here, take these two loaves of bread and this ham along, so that you won't starve."

*It was so hot inside that the Finn woman
helped Gerda off with her mittens and boots.
Otherwise the heat would have wilted her.*

When these provisions were tied on the back of the reindeer, the little robber girl opened the door and called in all the big dogs. Then she cut the tether with her knife and said to the reindeer, "Now run, but see that you take care of the little girl."

Gerda waved her big mittens to the little robber girl, and said goodbye. Then the reindeer bounded away, over stumps and stones, straight through the great forest, over swamps and across the plains, as fast as he could run. The wolves howled, the ravens shrieked, and—*ker-shew, ker-shew!*—the red streaks of light ripped through the heavens, with a noise that sounded like sneezing.

"Those are my old northern lights," said the reindeer. "See how they flash." And on he ran, faster than ever, by night and day. The loaves were eaten and the whole ham was eaten—and there they were in Lapland.

Sixth Story
The Lapp Woman and the Finn Woman

They stopped in front of a little hut, and a makeshift dwelling it was. The roof of it almost touched the ground, and the doorway was so low that the family had to lie on their stomachs and crawl in it or out of it. No one was at home except an old Lapp woman, who was cooking fish over a whale-oil lamp. The reindeer told her Gerda's whole story, but first he told his own, which he thought was much more important. Besides, Gerda was so cold that she couldn't say a thing.

"Oh, you poor creatures," the Lapp woman said, "you've still got such a long way to go. Why, you will have to travel hundreds of miles into Finnmark. For it's there that the Snow Queen is taking a country vacation, and burning her blue fireworks every evening. I'll jot down a message on a dried codfish, for I haven't any paper. I want you to take it to the Finn woman who lives up there. She will be able to tell you more about it than I can."

Living snowflakes swirled toward her.
They were monstrous and terrifying. They were the Snow Queen's
advance guard, and their shapes were most strange.

As soon as Gerda had thawed out, and had had something to eat and drink, the Lapp woman wrote a few words on a dried codfish, told Gerda to take good care of it, and tied her again on the back of the reindeer. Off he ran, and all night long the skies crackled and swished as the most beautiful northern lights flashed over their heads. At last they came to Finnmark, and knocked at the Finn woman's chimney, for she hadn't a sign of a door. It was so hot inside that the Finn woman went about almost naked. She was small and terribly dowdy, but she at once helped little Gerda off with her mittens and boots, and loosened her clothes. Otherwise the heat would have wilted her. Then the woman put a piece of ice on the reindeer's head, and read what was written on the codfish. She read it three times and when she knew it by heart, she put the fish into the kettle of soup, for they might as well eat it. She never wasted anything.

The reindeer told her his own story first, and then little Gerda's. The Finn woman winked a knowing eye, but she didn't say anything.

"You are such a wise woman," said the reindeer, "I know that you can tie all the winds of the world together with a bit of cotton thread. If the sailor unties one knot he gets a favorable wind. If he unties another he gets a stiff gale, while if he unties the third and fourth knots such a tempest rages that it flattens the trees in the forest. Won't you give this little girl something to drink that will make her as strong as twelve men, so that she may overpower the Snow Queen?"

"Twelve strong men," the Finn woman sniffled. "Much good that would be."

She went to the shelf, took down a big rolled-up skin, and unrolled it. On this skin strange characters were written, and the Finn woman read them until the sweat rolled down her forehead.

The reindeer again begged her to help Gerda, and little Gerda looked at her with such tearful, imploring eyes that the woman began winking again. She took the reindeer aside in a corner, and while she was putting another piece of ice on his head she whispered to him:

"Little Kay is indeed with the Snow Queen, and everything there just suits him fine. He thinks it is the best place in all the world, but that's because he has a splinter of glass in his heart and a small piece of it in his eye. Unless these can be gotten out, he will never be human again, and the Snow Queen will hold him in her power."

"But can't you fix little Gerda something to drink that will give her more power than all those things?"

"No power that I could give her could be as great as that which she already has. Don't you see how men and beasts are compelled to serve her, and how far she has come in the wide world since she started out in her naked feet? We mustn't tell her about this power. Strength lies in her heart, because she is such a sweet, innocent child. If she herself cannot reach the Snow Queen and rid little Kay of those pieces of glass, then there's no help that we can give her. The Snow Queen's garden lies about eight miles from here. You may carry the little girl there, and put her down by the big bush covered with red berries that grows in the snow. Then don't you stand there gossiping, but hurry to get back here."

The Finn woman lifted little Gerda onto the reindeer, and he galloped away as fast as he could.

"Oh!" cried Gerda, "I forgot my boots and I forgot my mittens." She soon felt the need of them in that knifelike cold, but the reindeer did not dare to stop. He galloped on until they came to the big bush that was covered with red berries. Here he set Gerda down and kissed her on the mouth while big shining tears ran down his face. Then he ran back as fast as he could. Little Gerda stood there without boots and without mittens, right in the middle of icy Finnmark.

She ran as fast as ever she could. A whole regiment of snowflakes swirled toward her, but they did not fall from the sky, for there was not a cloud up there, and the northern lights were ablaze.

Rank upon rank, the angels increased.
They struck the dreaded snowflakes with their lances
and slivered them into a thousand pieces.

The flakes skirmished along the ground, and the nearer they came the larger they grew. Gerda remembered how large and strange they had appeared when she looked at them under the magnifying glass. But here they were much more monstrous and terrifying. They were alive. They were the Snow Queen's advance guard, and their shapes were most strange. Some looked like ugly, overgrown porcupines. Some were like a knot of snakes that stuck out their heads in every direction, and others were like fat little bears with every hair a-bristle. All of them were glistening white, for all were living snowflakes.

It was so cold that, as little Gerda said the Lord's Prayer, she could see her breath freezing in front of her mouth, like a cloud of smoke. It grew thicker and thicker, and took the shape of little angels that grew bigger and bigger the moment they touched the ground. All of them had helmets on their heads and they carried shields and lances in their hands. Rank upon rank, they increased, and when Gerda had finished her prayer she was surrounded by a legion of angels. They struck the dread snowflakes with their lances and slivered them into a thousand pieces. Little Gerda walked on, unmolested and cheerful. The angels rubbed her hands and feet to make them warmer, and she trotted briskly along to the Snow Queen's palace.

But now let us see how little Kay was getting on. Little Gerda was furthest from his mind, and he hadn't the slightest idea that she was just outside the palace.

*The bits of glass made the word that
the Snow Queen had told Kay he must find
before he became his own master.*

Seventh Story
*What Happened in the Snow Queen's Palace,
and What Came of It*

The walls of the palace were driven snow. The windows and doors were the knife-edge wind. There were more than a hundred halls, shaped as the snow had drifted, and the largest of these extended for many a mile. All were lighted by the flare of the northern lights. All of the halls were so immense and so empty, so brilliant and so glacial! There was never a touch of gaiety in them; never so much as a little dance for the polar bears, at which the storm blast could have served for music, and the polar bears could have waddled about on their hind legs to show off their best manners. There was never a little party with such games as blind-bear's bluff or hide the paw-kerchief for the cubs, nor even a little afternoon coffee over which the white fox vixens could gossip. Empty, vast, and frigid were the Snow Queen's halls. The northern lights flared with such regularity that you could time exactly when they would be at the highest and lowest. In the middle of the vast, empty hall of snow was a frozen lake. It was cracked into a thousand pieces, but each piece was shaped so exactly like the others that it seemed a work of wonderful craftsmanship. The Snow Queen sat in the exact center of it when she was at home, and she spoke of this as sitting on her "Mirror of Reason." She said this mirror was the only one of its kind, and the best thing in all the world.

Little Kay was blue, yes, almost black, with the cold. But he did not feel it, because the Snow Queen had kissed away his icy tremblings, and his heart itself had almost turned to ice.

He was shifting some sharp, flat pieces of ice to and fro, trying to fit them into every possible pattern, for he wanted to make something with them. It was like the Chinese puzzle game that we play at home, juggling little flat pieces of wood about into special designs. Kay was cleverly arranging his pieces in the game of ice-cold reason. To him the patterns

Through the woods came riding a young girl
on a magnificent horse that Gerda recognized.
She was the little robber girl.

were highly remarkable and of the utmost importance, for the chip of glass in his eye made him see them that way. He arranged his pieces to spell out many words; but he could never find the way to make the one word he was so eager to form. The word was "Eternity." The Snow Queen had said to him, "If you can puzzle that out you shall be your own master, and I'll give you the whole world and a new pair of skates." But he could not puzzle it out.

"Now I am going to make a flying trip to the warm countries," the Snow Queen told him. "I want to go and take a look into the black cauldrons." She meant the volcanos of Etna and Vesuvius. "I must whiten them up a bit. They need it, and it will be such a relief after all those yellow lemons and purple grapes."

And away she flew. Kay sat all alone in that endless, empty, frigid hall, and puzzled over the pieces of ice until he almost cracked his skull. He sat so stiff and still that one might have thought he was frozen to death.

All of a sudden, little Gerda walked up to the palace through the great gate, which was a knife-edged wind. But Gerda said her evening prayer. The wind was lulled to rest, and the little girl came on into the vast, cold, empty hall. Then she saw Kay. She recognized him at once, and ran to throw her arms around him. She held him close and cried, "Kay! Dearest little Kay! I've found you at last!"

But he sat still, and stiff, and cold. Gerda shed hot tears, and when they fell upon him they went straight to his heart. They melted the lump of ice and burned away the splinter of glass in it. He looked up at her, and she sang:

"Where roses bloom so sweetly in the vale,
There shall you find the Christ Child,
without fail."

Kay burst into tears. He cried so freely that the little piece of glass in his eye was washed right out. "Gerda!" He knew her, and cried out in his happiness, "My sweet little Gerda, where have you been so long? And where have I been?" He looked around him and said, "How cold it is here! How enormous and empty!" He held fast to Gerda, who laughed until happy tears rolled down her cheeks. Their bliss was so heavenly that even the bits of glass danced about them and shared in their happiness. When the pieces grew tired, they dropped into a pattern that made the very word that the Snow Queen had told Kay he must find before he became his own master and received the whole world and a new pair of skates.

Gerda kissed his cheeks, and they turned pink again. She kissed his eyes, and they sparkled like hers. She kissed his hands and feet, and he became strong and well. The Snow Queen might come home now whenever she pleased, for there stood the order for Kay's release, written in letters of shining ice.

Hand in hand, Kay and Gerda strolled out of that enormous palace. They talked about Grandmother, and about the roses on their roof. Wherever they went, the wind died down and the sun shone out. When they came to the bush that was covered with red berries, the reindeer was waiting to meet them. He had brought along a young reindeer mate who had warm milk for the children to drink, and who kissed them on the mouth. Then these reindeer carried Gerda and Kay first to the Finn woman. They warmed themselves in her hot room, and when she had given them directions for their journey home they rode on to the Lapp woman. She had made them new clothes, and was ready to take them along in her sleigh.

Side by side, the reindeer ran with them to the limits of the north country, where the first green buds were to be seen. Here they said goodbye to the two reindeer and to the Lapp woman. "Farewell," they all said.

Now the first little birds began to chirp, and there were green buds all around them in the forest. Through the woods came riding a young girl on a magnificent horse that Gerda recognized, for it had once been harnessed to the golden carriage. The girl wore a bright red cap on her head, and a pair of pistols in her belt. She was the little robber girl, who had grown tired of staying at home, and who was setting out on a journey to the north country. If she didn't like it there, why, the world was wide, and there were many other places where she could go. She recognized Gerda at once, and Gerda knew her, too. It was a happy meeting.

"You're a fine one for gadding about," she told little Kay. "I'd just like to know whether you deserve to have someone running to the end of the earth for your sake."

But Gerda patted her cheek and asked about the prince and the princess.

"They are traveling in foreign lands," the girl told her.

"And the crow?"

"Oh, the crow is dead," she answered. "His tame ladylove is now a widow, and she wears a bit of black wool wrapped around her leg. She takes great pity on herself, but that's all stuff and nonsense. Now you tell me what has happened to you and how you caught up with Kay."

Gerda and Kay told her their story.

"Snip snap snurre, basse lurre," said the robber girl. "So everything came out all right." She shook them by the hand, and promised that if ever she passed through their town she would come to see them. And then she rode away.

Grandmother sat reading to them from her Bible.
And Kay and Gerda sat there, grown up,
but children still—children at heart.

Kay and Gerda held each other by the hand. And as they walked along they had wonderful spring weather. The land was green and strewn with flowers, church bells rang, and they saw the high steeples of a big town. It was the one where they used to live. They walked straight to Grandmother's house, and up the stairs, and into the room, where everything was just as it was when they left it. And the clock said *tick-tock*, and its hands were telling the time. But the moment they came in the door they noticed one change. They were grown up now.

The roses on the roof looked in at the open window, and their two

little stools were still out there. Kay and Gerda sat down on them, and held each other by the hand. Both of them had forgotten the icy, empty splendor of the Snow Queen's palace as completely as if it were some bad dream. Grandmother sat in God's good sunshine, reading to them from her Bible:

"Except ye become as little children, ye shall not enter into the Kingdom of Heaven."

Kay and Gerda looked into each other's eyes, and at last they understood the meaning of their old hymn:

"Where roses bloom so sweetly in the vale,
There shall you find the Christ Child,
without fail."

And they sat there, grown up, but children still—children at heart. And it was summer, warm, glorious summer.

The Ugly Duckling

"The book is selling like hot cakes!" declared Andersen in an 1843 letter translated by historian Maria Tatar. It was shortly after the release of his new collection, which included this popular, heartwarming tale. The similarities between Andersen's life and the ugly duckling's are irresistible: Andersen—gangly, poor, and uneducated—became a literary star despite the underestimation he suffered. In a similar fashion, the hatchling is mistaken for a common duck and mistreated before discovering that he is a beautiful swan. It took Andersen a year to write "The Ugly Duckling," and nineteen years later, he opened up about the process, calling the tale "the hardest to compose, perhaps because it was the most directly autobiographical." This classic example of an animal tale also spawned one of Andersen's famous quotes: "Being born in a duck yard does not matter, if only you are hatched from a swan's egg." In Andersen's day, the definition of artistic genius was shifting and was less bound to class than it had been before. He was part of an exciting new breed, and the tale's inspiring and hopeful message continues to make it one of Andersen's most beloved stories to this day.—ND

Color lithographs by Theo van Hoytema, Dutch, 1893

From the manor walls down to the water,
burdock leaves grew. In this wilderness,
a duck sat on her nest, hatching her ducklings.

t was so beautiful out in the country. It was summer—the wheat fields were golden, the oats were green, and down among the green meadows the hay was stacked. There the stork minced about on his red legs, clacking away in Egyptian, which was the language his mother had taught him. Round about the field and meadowlands rose vast forests, in which deep lakes lay hidden. Yes, it was indeed lovely out there in the country.

In the midst of the sunshine there stood an old manor house that had a deep moat around it. From the walls of the manor right down to the water's edge great burdock leaves grew, and there were some so tall that little children could stand upright beneath the biggest of them. In this wilderness of leaves, which was as dense as the forest itself, a duck sat on her nest, hatching her ducklings. She was becoming somewhat weary, because sitting is such a dull business and scarcely anyone came to see her. The other ducks would much rather swim in the moat than waddle out and squat under a burdock leaf to gossip with her.

But at last the eggshells began to crack, one after another. "Peep, peep!" said the little things, as they came to life and poked out their heads.

"Quack, quack!" said the duck, and quick as quick can be they all waddled out to have a look at the green world under the leaves. Their mother let them look as much as they pleased, because green is good for the eyes.

But at last the eggshells began to crack.
"Peep, peep!" said the little things,
as they came to life and poked out their heads.

At last the big egg did crack.
"Peep," said the young one, and out he tumbled,
but he was so big and ugly.

"How wide the world is," said all the young ducks, for they certainly had much more room now than they had when they were in their eggshells.

"Do you think this is the whole world?" their mother asked. "Why, it extends on and on, clear across to the other side of the garden and right on into the parson's field, though that is further than I have ever been. I do hope you are all hatched," she said as she got up. "No, not quite all. The biggest egg still lies here. How much longer is this going to take? I am really rather tired of it all," she said, but she settled back on her nest.

"Well, how goes it?" asked an old duck who came to pay her a call.

"It's taking a long time with that one egg," said the duck on the nest.

"It won't crack, but look at the others. They are the cutest little ducklings I've ever seen. They look exactly like their father, the wretch! He hasn't come to see me at all."

"Let's have a look at the egg that won't crack," the old duck said. "It's a turkey egg, and you can take my word for it. I was fooled like that once myself. What trouble and care I had with those turkey children, for I may as well tell you, they are afraid of the water. I simply could not get them into it. I quacked and snapped at them, but it wasn't a bit of

*Next day the mother led her whole family
down to the moat. "Quack, quack," said she,
and one duckling after another plunged in.*

The poor duckling, who looked so ugly,
was pecked and pushed and made fun of by the ducks,
and the chickens as well.

use. Let me see the egg. Certainly, it's a turkey egg. Let it lie, and go teach your other children how to swim."

"Oh, I'll sit a little longer. I've been at it so long already that I may as well sit here half the summer."

"Suit yourself," said the old duck, and away she waddled.

At last the big egg did crack. "Peep," said the young one, and out he tumbled, but he was so big and ugly.

The duck took a look at him. "That's a frightfully big duckling," she said. "He doesn't look the least like the others. Can he really be a turkey baby? Well, well! I'll soon find out. Into the water he shall go, even if I have to shove him in myself."

Next day the weather was perfectly splendid, and the sun shone down on all the green burdock leaves. The mother duck led her whole family down to the moat. *Splash!* She took to the water. "Quack, quack," said she, and one duckling after another plunged in. The water went over their heads, but they came up in a flash, and floated to perfection. Their legs worked automatically, and they were all there in the water. Even the big, ugly gray one was swimming along.

"Why, that's no turkey," she said. "See how nicely he uses his legs, and how straight he holds himself. He's my very own son after all, and quite good-looking if you look at him properly. Quack, quack, come with me. I'll lead you out into the world and introduce you to the duck yard. But keep close to me so that you won't get stepped on, and watch out for the cat!"

Thus they sallied into the duck yard, where all was in an uproar because two families were fighting over the head of an eel. But the cat got it, after all.

"You see, that's the way of the world." The mother duck licked her bill because she wanted the eel's head for herself. "Stir your legs. Bustle about, and mind that you bend your necks to that old duck over there. She's the noblest of us all, and has Spanish blood in her. That's why she's so fat.

So he ran away, and he flew over the fence.
The little birds in the bushes darted up in a fright.

See that red rag around her leg? That's a wonderful thing, and the highest distinction a duck can get. It shows that they don't want to lose her, and that she's to have special attention from man and beast. Shake yourselves! Don't turn your toes in. A well-bred duckling turns his toes way out, just as his father and mother do—this way. So then! Now duck your necks and say quack!"

They did as she told them, but the other ducks around them looked on and said right out loud, "See here! Must we have this brood too, just as if there weren't enough of us already? And—fie! What an ugly-looking fellow that duckling is! We won't stand for him." One duck charged up and bit his neck.

"Let him alone," his mother said. "He isn't doing any harm."

"Possibly not," said the duck who bit him, "but he's too big and strange, and therefore he needs a good whacking."

"What nice-looking children you have, Mother," said the old duck with the rag around her leg. "They are all pretty except that one. He didn't come out so well. It's a pity you can't hatch him again."

"That can't be managed, your ladyship," said the mother. "He isn't so handsome, but he's as good as can be, and he swims just as well as the rest,

The ganders said,
"You're so ugly that we have taken a fancy to you.
Come with us and be a bird of passage.

or, I should say, even a little better than they do. I hope his looks will improve with age, and after awhile, he won't seem so big. He took too long in the egg, and that's why his figure isn't all that it should be." She pinched his neck and preened his feathers. "Moreover, he's a drake, so it won't matter so much. I think he will be quite strong, and I'm sure he will amount to something."

"The other ducklings are pretty enough," said the old duck. "Now make yourselves right at home, and if you find an eel's head you may bring it to me."

So they felt quite at home. But the poor duckling who had been the last one out of his egg, and who looked so ugly, was pecked and pushed about and made fun of by the ducks, and the chickens as well. "He's too big," they all said. The turkey gobbler, who thought himself an emperor because he was born wearing spurs, puffed up like a ship under full sail and bore down upon him, gobbling and gobbling until he was red in the face. The poor duckling did not know where he dared stand

They were quick to notice the strange duckling.
The cat began to purr, and the hen began to cluck.
"What on earth!" said the old woman.

or where he dared walk. He was so sad because he was so desperately ugly, and because he was the laughing stock of the whole barnyard.

So it went on the first day, and after that things went from bad to worse. The poor duckling was chased and buffeted about by everyone. Even his own brothers and sisters abused him. "Oh," they would always say, "how we wish the cat would catch you, you ugly thing." And his mother said, "How I do wish you were miles away." The ducks nipped him, and the hens pecked him, and the girl who fed them kicked him with her foot.

So he ran away; and he flew over the fence. The little birds in the bushes darted up in a fright. "That's because I'm so ugly," he thought, and closed his eyes, but he ran on just the same until he reached the great marsh where the wild ducks lived. There he lay all night long, weary and disheartened.

When morning came, the wild ducks flew up to have a look at their new companion. "What sort of creature are you?" they asked, as the duckling turned in all directions, bowing his best to all of them. "You are terribly ugly," they told him, "but that's nothing to us so long as you don't marry into our family."

Poor duckling! Marriage certainly had never entered his mind. All he wanted was for them to let him lie among the reeds and drink a little water from the marsh.

There he stayed for two whole days. Then he met two wild geese, or rather wild ganders—for they were males. They had not been out of the shell very long, and that's what made them so sure of themselves.

"Say there, comrade," they said, "you're so ugly that we have taken a fancy to you. Come with us and be a bird of passage. In another marsh near by, there are some fetching wild geese, all nice young ladies who know how to quack. You are so ugly that you'll completely turn their heads."

Bing! Bang! Shots rang in the air, and these two ganders fell dead among the reeds. The water was red with their blood. *Bing! Bang!* The shots rang, and as whole flocks of wild geese flew up from the reeds another volley crashed. A great hunt was in progress. The hunters lay under cover all around the marsh, and some even perched on branches of trees that overhung the reeds. Blue smoke rose like clouds from the shade of the trees, and drifted far out over the water.

The bird dogs came—*splash, splash!*—through the swamp, bending down the reeds and the rushes on every side. This gave the poor duckling such a fright that he twisted his head about to hide it under his wing. But at that very moment a fearfully big dog appeared right beside him. His tongue lolled out of his mouth and his wicked eyes glared horribly. He opened his wide jaws, flashed his sharp teeth, and—*splash, splash!*—on he went without touching the duckling.

"Thank heavens," he sighed, "I'm so ugly that the dog won't even bother to bite me."

He lay perfectly still, while the bullets splattered through the reeds as shot after shot was fired. It was late in the day before things became quiet again, and even then the poor duckling didn't dare move. He waited several hours before he ventured to look about him, and then he

One evening as the sun was setting,
a great flock of large, handsome swans appeared.
The duckling had never seen birds so beautiful.

scurried away from that marsh as fast as he could go. He ran across field and meadows. The wind was so strong that he had to struggle to keep his feet.

Late in the evening he came to a miserable little hovel, so ramshackle that it did not know which way to tumble, and that was the only reason it still stood. The wind struck the duckling so hard that the poor little fellow had to sit down on his tail to withstand it. The storm blew stronger and stronger, but the duckling noticed that one hinge had come loose and the door hung so crooked that he could squeeze through the crack into the room, and that's just what he did.

Here lived an old woman with her cat and her hen. The cat, whom she called "Sonny," could arch his back, purr, and even make sparks, though for that you had to stroke his fur the wrong way. The hen had short little legs, so she was called "Chickey Shortleg." She laid good eggs, and the old woman loved her as if she had been her own child.

In the morning they were quick to notice the strange duckling. The cat began to purr, and the hen began to cluck.

"What on earth!" The old woman looked around, but she was nearsighted, and she mistook the duckling for a fat duck that had lost its way. "That was a good catch," she said. "Now I shall have duck eggs—unless it's a drake. We must try it out." So the duckling was tried out for three weeks, but not one egg did he lay.

In this house the cat was master and the hen was mistress. They always said, "We and the world," for they thought themselves half of the world, and much the better half at that. The duckling thought that there might be more than one way of thinking, but the hen would not hear of it.

"Can you lay eggs?" she asked.

"No."

"Then be so good as to hold your tongue."

The cat asked, "Can you arch your back, purr, or make sparks?"

"No."

"Then keep your opinion to yourself when sensible people are talking."

The duckling sat in a corner, feeling most despondent. Then he remembered the fresh air and the sunlight. Such a desire to go swimming on the water possessed him that he could not help telling the hen about it.

"What on earth has come over you?" the hen cried. "You haven't a thing to do, and that's why you get such silly notions. Lay us an egg, or learn to purr, and you'll get over it."

"But it's so refreshing to float on the water," said the duckling, "so refreshing to feel it rise over your head as you dive to the bottom."

"Yes, it must be a great pleasure!" said the hen. "I think you must have gone crazy. Ask the cat, who's the wisest fellow I know, whether he likes to swim or dive down in the water. Of myself I say nothing. But ask the old woman, our mistress. There's no one on earth wiser than she is. Do you imagine she wants to go swimming and feel the water rise over her head?"

"You don't understand me," said the duckling.

"Well, if we don't, who would? Surely you don't think you are cleverer than the cat and the old woman—to say nothing of myself. Don't be so

What did he see mirrored in the stream?
He himself was a swan! Being born in a duck yard does not matter,
if only you are hatched from a swan's egg.

conceited, child. Just thank your Maker for all the kindness we have shown you. Didn't you get into this snug room, and fall in with people who can tell you what's what? But you are such a numbskull that it's no pleasure to have you around. Believe me, I tell you this for your own good. I say unpleasant truths, but that's the only way you can know who are your friends. Be sure now that you lay some eggs. See to it that you learn to purr or to make sparks."

"I think I'd better go out into the wide world," said the duckling.

"Suit yourself," said the hen.

So off went the duckling. He swam on the water, and dived down in it, but still he was slighted by every living creature because of his ugliness.

Autumn came on. The leaves in the forest turned yellow and brown. The wind took them and whirled them about. The heavens looked cold as the low clouds hung heavy with snow and hail. Perched on the fence, the raven screamed, "Caw, caw!" and trembled with cold. It made one shiver to think of it. Pity the poor little duckling!

One evening, just as the sun was setting in splendor, a great flock of large, handsome birds appeared out of the reeds. The duckling had never seen birds so beautiful. They were dazzling white, with long graceful necks. They were swans. They uttered a very strange cry as they unfurled their magnificent wings to fly from this cold land, away to warmer countries and to open waters. They went up so high, so very high, that the ugly little duckling felt a strange uneasiness come over him as he watched them. He went around and around in the water, like a wheel. He craned his neck to follow their course, and gave a cry so shrill and strange that he frightened himself. Oh! He could not forget them—those splendid, happy birds. When he could no longer see them he dived to the very bottom, and when he came up again he was quite beside himself. He did not know what birds they were or whither they were bound, yet he loved them more than anything he had ever loved before. It was not that he envied them, for how could

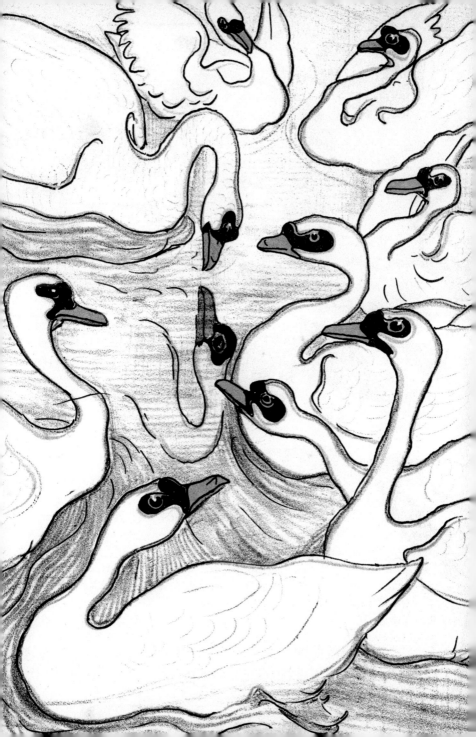

Several little children came into the garden
to throw bits of bread upon the water.
The smallest child cried, "Here's a new one!"

he ever dare dream of wanting their marvelous beauty for himself? He would have been grateful if only the ducks would have tolerated him—the poor ugly creature.

The winter grew cold—so bitterly cold that the duckling had to swim to and fro in the water to keep it from freezing over. But every night the hole in which he swam kept getting smaller and smaller. Then it froze so hard that the duckling had to paddle continuously to keep the crackling ice from closing in upon him. At last, too tired to move, he was frozen fast in the ice.

Early that morning a farmer came by, and when he saw how things were he went out on the pond, broke away the ice with his wooden shoe, and carried the duckling home to his wife. There the duckling revived, but when the children wished to play with him he thought they meant to hurt him. Terrified, he fluttered into the milk pail, splashing the whole room with milk. The woman shrieked and threw up her hands as he flew into the butter tub, and then in and out of the meal barrel. Imagine what he looked like now! The woman screamed and lashed out at him with fire tongs. The children tumbled over each other as they tried to catch him, and they laughed and they shouted. Luckily the door was open, and the duckling escaped through it into the bushes, where he lay down, in the newly fallen snow, as if in a daze.

But it would be too sad to tell of all the hardships and wretchedness he had to endure during this cruel winter. When the warm sun shone once more, the duckling was still alive among the reeds of the marsh. The larks began to sing again. It was beautiful springtime.

Then, quite suddenly, he lifted his wings. They swept through the air much more strongly than before, and their powerful strokes carried him far. Before he quite knew what was happening, he found himself in a great garden where apple trees bloomed. The lilacs filled the air with sweet scent and hung in clusters from long, green branches that bent over a winding stream. Oh, but it was lovely here in the freshness of spring!

From the thicket before him came three lovely white swans. They ruffled their feathers and swam lightly in the stream. The duckling recognized these noble creatures, and a strange feeling of sadness came upon him.

"I shall fly near these royal birds, and they will peck me to bits because I, who am so very ugly, dare to go near them. But I don't care. Better be killed by them than be nipped by the ducks, pecked by the hens, kicked about by the hen-yard girl, or suffer such misery in winter."

So he flew into the water and swam toward the splendid swans. They saw him, and swept down upon him with their rustling feathers raised. "Kill me!" said the poor creature, and he bowed his head down over the water to wait for death. But what did he see there, mirrored in the clear stream? He beheld his own image, and it was no longer the reflection of a clumsy, dirty, gray bird, ugly and offensive. He himself was a swan! Being born in a duck yard does not matter, if only you are hatched from a swan's egg.

He felt quite glad that he had come through so much trouble and misfortune, for now he had a fuller understanding of his own good fortune, and of beauty when he met with it. The great swans swam all around him and stroked him with their bills.

The old swans bowed in his honor.
Then he felt bashful, and tucked his head under his wing.
He did not know what this was all about.

Several little children came into the garden to throw grain and bits of bread upon the water. The smallest child cried, "Here's a new one!" and the others rejoiced, "Yes, a new one has come." They clapped their hands, danced around, and ran to bring their father and mother.

And they threw bread and cake upon the water, while they all agreed, "The new one is the most handsome of all. He's so young and so good-looking." The old swans bowed in his honor.

Then he felt very bashful, and tucked his head under his wing. He did not know what this was all about. He felt so very happy, but he wasn't at all proud, for a good heart never grows proud. He thought about how he had been persecuted and scorned, and now he heard them all call him the most beautiful of all beautiful birds. The lilacs dipped their clusters into the stream before him, and the sun shone so warm and so heartening. He rustled his feathers and held his slender neck high, as he cried out with full heart: "I never dreamed there could be so much happiness, when I was the ugly duckling."

The Tinderbox

"Aren't you every inch a soldier!" fawns a witch as she butters up a soldier return-
ing from war, enlisting him to fetch her a magic tinderbox from a spooky subter-
ranean cavern. To modern-day readers, this almost-two-hundred-year-old mer-
cenary with knapsack and sword may seem old-fashioned. But, in fact, he is one
of the folkloric forefathers of the modern-day action hero. The brassy self-reli-
ance of the soldier in this famous tale from 1835 makes him the perfect anti-
authoritarian foil. But it's the soldier's self-interested actions and the story's lack
of clear moral messages that riled critics looking for child-friendly fare when
the tale first appeared. Like the soldier, observes historian Bengt Holbek, Andersen was encouraged by his father "to rely on himself and go out into the great
wide world to seek his fortune." Andersen's father had been devoted to him, and
they often read one of their favorite books together, *The Thousand and One
Nights*, whose tale "Aladdin" is echoed here, as is an oral tale from Andersen's
youth, "The Spirit in the Candle," in which a soldier refuses to hand over a magic
candle. Andersen's tale, which melds a wide range of folkloric motifs in a new
way, is hailed today as a masterpiece.—ND

Watercolors and black-and-white drawings by Heinrich Strub, Swiss, 1956

"See that big tree?" The witch pointed.
"Climb to the top of the trunk and you'll find a hole through
which you can let yourself down deep under the tree."

here came a soldier marching down the high road—*one, two, one, two!* He had his knapsack on his back and his sword at his side as he came home from the wars. On the road he met a witch, an ugly old witch, a witch whose lower lip dangled right down on her chest.

"Good evening, soldier," she said. "What a fine sword you've got there, and what a big knapsack. Aren't you every inch a soldier! And now you shall have money, as much as you please."

"That's very kind, you old witch," said the soldier.

"See that big tree?" The witch pointed to one near by them. "It's hollow to the roots. Climb to the top of the trunk and you'll find a hole through which you can let yourself down deep under the tree. I'll tie a rope around your middle, so that when you call me I can pull you up again."

"What would I do deep down under that tree?" the soldier wanted to know.

"Fetch money," the witch said. "Listen. When you touch the bottom you'll find yourself in a great hall. It is very bright there, because hundreds of lamps are burning. By their light you will see three doors. Each door has a key in it, so you can open them all.

"If you walk into the first room, you'll see a large chest in the middle of the floor. On it sits a dog, and his eyes are as big as saucers. But don't worry about that. I'll give you my blue checked apron to spread out on the floor. Snatch up that dog and set him on my apron. Then you can open the chest and take out as many coins as you please. They are all copper.

"But if silver suits you better, then go into the next room. There sits a dog, and his eyes are as big as mill wheels. But don't you care about that. Set the dog on my apron while you line your pockets with silver.

"Maybe you'd rather have gold. You can, you know. You can have all the gold you can carry if you go into the third room. The only hitch is that there on the money chest sits a dog, and each of his eyes is as big as the Round

The soldier slid through the hole in the tree,
down into the great hall where hundreds of lamps were burning.

PAGES **176/177** *He made for the second room.*
There sat the dog with eyes as big as mill wheels.
"Don't you look at me like that," he said.

Tower of Copenhagen. That's the sort of dog he is. But never you mind how fierce he looks. Just set him on my apron and he'll do you no harm as you help yourself from the chest to all the gold you want."

"That suits me," said the soldier. "But what do you get out of all this, you old witch? I suppose that you want your share."

"No indeed," said the witch. "I don't want a penny of it. All I ask is for you to fetch me an old tinderbox that my grandmother forgot the last time she was down there."

"Good," said the soldier. "Tie the rope around me."

"Here it is," said the witch, "and here's my blue checked apron."

The soldier climbed up to the hole in the nearest tree and let himself slide through it, feet foremost, down into the great hall where the hundreds of lamps were burning, just as the witch had said. Now he threw open the first door he came to. Ugh! There sat a dog glaring at him with eyes as big as saucers.

"You're a nice fellow," the soldier said, as he shifted him to the witch's apron and took all the copper coins that his pockets would hold. He shut up the chest, set the dog back on it, and made for the second room. Alas and alack! There sat the dog with eyes as big as mill wheels.

"Don't you look at me like that." The soldier set him on the witch's apron. "You're apt to strain your eyesight." When he saw the chest brimful of silver, he threw away all his coppers and filled both his pockets and knapsack with silver alone. Then he went into the third room. Oh, what a horrible sight to see! The dog in there really did have eyes as big as the Round Tower, and when he rolled them they spun like wheels.

"Good evening," the soldier said, and saluted, for such a dog he had never seen before. But on second glance he thought to himself, "This won't do." So he lifted the dog down to the floor, and threw open the chest. What a sight! Here was gold and to spare. He could buy out all Copenhagen with it. He could buy all the cake woman's sugar pigs, and all the tin soldiers,

whips, and rocking horses there are in the world. Yes, *there* was really money!

In short order the soldier got rid of all the silver coins he had stuffed in his pockets and knapsack, to put gold in their place. Yes, sir, he crammed all his pockets, his knapsack, his cap, and his boots so full that he scarcely could walk. Now he was made of money. After putting the dog back on the chest, he banged out the door and called up through the hollow tree:

"Pull me up now, you old witch."

"Have you got the tinderbox?" asked the witch.

"Confound the tinderbox," the soldier shouted. "I clean forgot it."

When he fetched it, the witch hauled him up. There he stood on the high road again, with his pockets, boots, knapsack, and cap full of gold.

"What do you want with the tinderbox?" he asked the old witch.

"None of your business," she told him. "You have had your money, so hand over my tinderbox."

"Nonsense," said the soldier. "I'll take out my sword and I'll cut your head off if you don't tell me at once what you want with it."

"I won't," the witch screamed at him.

So he cut her head off. There she lay! But he tied all his money in her apron, slung it over his shoulder, stuck the tinderbox in his pocket, and struck out for town.

It was a splendid town. He took the best rooms at the best inn, and ordered all the good things he liked to eat, for he was a rich man now because

"Go get me some money," he ordered.
Zip! *The dog was gone.* Zip! *He was back again,*
with a bag full of copper in his mouth.

he had so much money. The servant who cleaned his boots may have thought them remarkably well worn for a man of such means, but that was before he went shopping. Next morning he bought boots worthy of him, and the best clothes. Now that he had turned out to be such a fashionable gentleman, people told him all about the splendors of their town—all about their king, and what a pretty princess he had for a daughter.

"Where can I see her?" the soldier inquired.

"You can't see her at all," everyone said. "She lives in a great copper castle inside all sorts of walls and towers. Only the king can come in or go out of it, for it's been foretold that the princess will marry a common soldier. The king would much rather she didn't."

"I'd like to see her just the same," the soldier thought. But there was no way to manage it.

Now he lived a merry life. He went to the theater, drove about in the king's garden, and gave away money to poor people. This was to his credit, for he remembered from the old days what it feels like to go without a penny in your pocket. Now that he was wealthy and well dressed, he had all too many who called him their friend and a genuine gentleman. That pleased him.

But he spent money every day without making any, and wound up with only two coppers to his name. He had to quit his fine quarters to live in a garret, clean his own boots, and mend them himself with a darning needle. None of his friends came to see him, because there were too many stairs to climb.

One evening when he sat in the dark without even enough money to buy a candle, he suddenly remembered there was a candle end in the tinderbox that he had picked up when the witch sent him down the hollow tree. He got out the tinderbox, and the moment he struck sparks from the flint of it his door burst open and there stood a dog from down under the tree. It was the one with eyes as big as saucers.

PAGES 180/181 *Next morning when the king and queen were drinking their tea, the princess told them her dream about a dog and about a soldier who had kissed her.*

"What," said the dog, "is my lord's command?"

"What's this?" said the soldier. "Have I got the sort of tinderbox that will get me whatever I want? Go get me some money," he ordered the dog. *Zip!* The dog was gone. *Zip!* He was back again, with a bag full of copper in his mouth.

Now the soldier knew what a remarkable tinderbox he had. Strike it once and there was the dog from the chest of copper coins. Strike it twice and here came the dog who had the silver. Three times brought the dog who guarded gold.

Back went the soldier to his comfortable quarters. Out strode the soldier in fashionable clothes. Immediately his friends knew him again, because they liked him so much.

Then the thought occurred to him, "Isn't it odd that no one ever gets to see the princess? They say she's very pretty, but what's the good of it as long as she stays locked up in that large copper castle with so many towers? Why can't I see her? Where's my tinderbox?" He struck a light and—*zip!*—came the dog with eyes as big as saucers.

"It certainly is late," said the soldier. "Practically midnight. But I do want a glimpse of the princess, if only for a moment."

Out the door went the dog, and faster than the soldier could believe, here came the dog with the princess on his back. She was sound asleep, and so pretty that anyone could see she was a princess. The soldier couldn't keep from kissing her, because he was every inch a soldier. Then the dog took the princess home.

Next morning when the king and queen were drinking their tea, the princess told them about the strange dream she'd had—all about a dog and a soldier. She'd ridden on the dog's back, and the soldier had kissed her.

"Now that was a fine story," said the queen. The next night one of the old ladies of the court was under orders to sit by the princess's bed, and see whether this was a dream or something else altogether. The soldier

*"Don't!" cried the king, but the biggest dog
took him and the queen too,
and tossed them up after the others.*

was longing to see the pretty princess again, so the dog
came by night to take her up and away as fast as he could
run. But the old lady pulled on her storm boots and ran
right after them. When she saw them disappear into
a large house she thought, "Now I know where it is,"
and drew a big cross on the door with a piece of chalk.
Then she went home to bed, and before long the dog
brought the princess home, too. But when the dog saw
that cross marked on the soldier's front door, he got
himself a piece of chalk and cross-marked every door
in the town. This was a clever thing to do, because now
the old lady couldn't tell the right door from all the
wrong doors he had marked.

Early in the morning along came the king and
queen, the old lady, and all the officers, to see where
the princess had been.

"Here it is," said the king when he saw the first cross
mark.

"No, my dear. There it is," said the queen, who was looking next door.

"Here's one, there's one, and yonder's another one!" they all said. Wherever they looked they saw chalk marks, so they gave up searching. The queen, though, was an uncommonly clever woman, who could do more than ride in a coach. She took her big gold scissors, cut out a piece of silk, and made a neat little bag. She filled it with fine buckwheat flour and tied it onto the princess's back. Then she pricked a little hole in it so that the flour would sift out along the way, wherever the princess might go.

Again the dog came in the night, took the princess on his back, and ran with her to the soldier, who loved her so much that he would have been glad to be a prince just so he could make her his wife.

The dog didn't notice how the flour made a trail from the castle right up to the soldier's window, where he ran up the wall with the princess. So in the morning it was all too plain to the king and queen just where their daughter had been.

They took the soldier and they put him in prison. There he sat. It

They put the soldier in the king's carriage.
All three dogs danced in front of it,
and the princess came out to be queen.

was dark, and it was dismal, and they told him, "Tomorrow is the day for you to hang." That didn't cheer him up any, and as for his tinderbox, he'd left it behind at the inn. In the morning he could see through his narrow little window how the people all hurried out of town to see him hanged. He heard the drums beat and he saw the soldiers march. In the crowd of running people he saw a shoemaker's boy in a leather apron and slippers. The boy galloped so fast that off flew one slipper, which hit the wall right where the soldier pressed his face to the iron bars.

"Hey there, you shoemaker's boy, there's no hurry," the soldier shouted. "Nothing can happen till I get there. But if you run to where I live and bring me my tinderbox, I'll give you four coppers. Put your best foot foremost."

The shoemaker's boy could use four coppers, so he rushed the tinderbox to the soldier, and—well, now we shall hear what happened!

Outside the town a high gallows had been built. Around it stood soldiers and hundreds of thousands of people. The king and queen sat on a splendid throne, opposite the judge and the whole council. The soldier already stood upon the ladder, but just as they were about to put the rope around his neck he said the custom was to grant a poor criminal one last small favor. He wanted to smoke a pipe of tobacco—the last he'd ever be smoking in this world.

The king couldn't refuse him, so the soldier struck fire from his tinderbox, once—twice—and a third time. *Zip!* There stood all the dogs, one with eyes as big as saucers, one with eyes as big as mill wheels, one with eyes as big as the Round Tower of Copenhagen.

"Help me. Save me from hanging!" said the soldier. Those dogs took the judges and all the council, some by the leg and some by the nose, and tossed them so high that they came down broken to bits.

"Don't!" cried the king, but the biggest dog took him and the queen too, and tossed them up after the others. Then the soldiers trembled and the people shouted, "Soldier, be our king and marry the pretty princess."

So they put the soldier in the king's carriage. All three of his dogs danced in front of it, and shouted "Hurrah!" The boys whistled through their fingers, and the soldiers saluted. The princess came out of the copper castle to be queen, and that suited her exactly. The wedding lasted an entire week, and the three dogs sat at the table, with their eyes opened wider than ever before.

Image Credits by Source

©**Laura Barrett**, London (Art Direction by Noel Daniel): see Image Credits by Artist for page numbers

The Collection of Kendra and Allan Daniel; photography by Gavin Ashworth: 190

©**Evangelische Kirchengemeinde Dettenhausen**, Dettenhausen, Germany: 52, 63, 65, 72

Hans Christian Andersen Museum, Odense, Denmark: 19 top left and top right

The Hans Christian Andersen Museum, Solvang, California: 2, 8 top left and top right

©**1981 NordSüd Verlag AG**, CH-8005, Zurich, Switzerland; *Die kleine Seejungfrau,* illustrations by Josef Paleček: 51, 55–60, 66–71, 75–83

©**Okaya City**, Nagano Prefecture, Japan: 16

©**Penguin Group (USA) Inc.**, *The Snow Queen* by Hans Christian Andersen, illustrated by K. Beverley and E. Ellender, ©1929 E.P. Dutton & Co., Inc., renewed ©1957 E.P. Dutton & Co., Inc. Used by permission of Dutton Children's Books, a division of Penguin Group (USA) Inc.: 11, 105–149

Princeton University Library, Cotsen Children's Library, Department of Rare Books and Special Collections: 33–47

©**Tom Seidmann-Freud**: Front cover, 21, 28–29

©**Heinrich Strub**: 173–185

Unless otherwise noted, the remaining images come from private collections.

Image Credits by Artist

HCA **Hans Christian Andersen**: 19 top left and top right

LB **Laura Barrett** (Art Direction by Noel Daniel): 26–27, 30, 85, 88, 92, 95, 99, 102–103, 151, 171

JB **Johanna Beckmann**: 31, 150

KB **Katharine Beverley**: 11, 105–149

EVB **Eleanor Vere Boyle**: 2, 8 top left

HC **Harry Clarke**: 87, 91

EE **Elizabeth Ellender**: 11, 105–149

JH **Jennie Harbour**: 22

GIN **Georgi Iwanowitsch Narbut**: 33–47

KN **Kay Nielsen**: 4, 6, 8 top right, 13, 24 (detail), 97, 100, 190

JP **Josef Paleček**: 51, 55–60, 66–71, 75–83

AR **Arthur Rackham**: 1, 48 (amended), 49 (detail), 84

KR **Käthe Reine**: 94, 170

LR **Lotte Reiniger**: 52, 63, 65, 72

TSF **Tom Seidmann-Freud**: Front cover, 21, 28–29

HS **Heinrich Strub**: 173–185

TT **Takeo Takei**: 16

TVH **Theo van Hoytema**: 14, 152–169

Silhouette Credits by Page Number

Please see center column for the key to
the artists' intitials.

Page 1: AR. *Introduction*: **19** top left and top
right: HCA. *The Tales*: **24**: KN. *The Princess and
the Pea*: **26–27**: LB. *The Nightingale*: **30**: LB. **31**:
JB. **33–47**: GIN. *The Little Mermaid*: **48–49**: AR.
52, 63, 65, 72: LR. *The Emperor's New Clothes*:
84: AR. **85, 88, 92**: LB. *The Steadfast Tin
Soldier*: **94**: KR. **95, 99**: LB. *The Snow Queen*:
102–103: LB. *The Ugly Duckling*: **150**: JB. **151**:
LB. *The Tinderbox*: **170**: KR. **171**: LB.

About the Editor

TASCHEN editor Noel Daniel graduated from Princeton University and studied in Berlin on a Fulbright Scholarship. She earned a master's degree in London and served as director of a photography art gallery before becoming a book editor. Her TASCHEN books to date include *A Treasury of Wintertime Tales*, *The Fairy Tales of Hans Christian Andersen*, *The Fairy Tales of the Brothers Grimm*, *Magic 1400s– 1950s*, and *The Circus 1870s–1950s*.

Acknowledgments

I would especially like to thank my husband and collaborator, Andy Disl, one of the art directors at TASCHEN and the designer of this book, for his generosity, ease, and humor, and his unique ability to offer the best graphic interpretation of an idea. I would also like to give very special thanks to the publisher Benedikt Taschen for his encouragement and generous support of this project.

Special thanks also go to the illustrator Laura Barrett, who is a pleasure to work with and whose collaboration and professionalism were gifts to this project. I would also like to thank Mallory Farrugia for her excellent editorial assistance and Jessica Hoffmann for her fine copyediting.

Many thanks also to Doug Adrianson, Lottie Arnold, Gavin Ashworth, Alex and Bruce Bacon, Tyler and Wilson Bacon, Davara Bennett, Solveig Brunholm, Madeline Bryant, Susanna Cantor, Kendra and Allan Daniel, Margery and Tom Daniel, Perry Daniel, Nemuel DePaula, Stephanie Derbyshire, Ayala Drori, Edda Eckhardt, Colin Enriquez, Evangelische Kirchengemeinde Dettenhausen, Sherri Feldman, Charles Greene, Ed Gregory, Alfred Happ, Amnon Harari, Asaf Harari, Michael Hendricks, ILF Douga Museum in Okaya, Ryugo Imai, Andrea L. Immel, Luke Ingram, Mika Kasai, Barbara Maurer, Connie Melendez, Kathy Mullins, Kathrin Murr, Horst Neuzner, Jennifer Patrick, AnnaLee Pauls, Christian R. Ragni, Jordan Romanoff, Reid Rutledge, Jonas Scheler, Anna Skinner, Heinrich Strub, Mary Sullivan, Mitsuko Ueshima, Annick Volk, Yoshiro Yamagishi, Marco Zivny.

For our son, Cyrus Daniel-Disl

EACH AND EVERY TASCHEN BOOK PLANTS A SEED!
TASCHEN is a carbon neutral publisher. Each year, we offset our annual carbon
emissions with carbon credits at the Instituto Terra, a reforestation program in
Minas Gerais, Brazil, founded by Lélia and Sebastião Salgado. To find out more about
this ecological partnership, please check: www.taschen.com/zerocarbon
Inspiration: unlimited. Carbon footprint: zero.

To stay informed about TASCHEN and our upcoming titles, please subscribe to
our free magazine at www.taschen.com/magazine, follow us on Twitter, Instagram,
and Facebook, or e-mail your questions to contact@taschen.com.

© 2017 TASCHEN GmbH
Hohenzollernring 53, D–50672, Köln
www.taschen.com

Translations by Danish-born Jean Hersholt (1886–1956), a Hollywood actor and
radio star who dedicated years of his life to translating all of Andersen's tales from
the original Danish. His English translations were first published in 1942
(© MBI, Inc., reproduced with the permission of MBI, Inc.).
Cover designed by Andy Disl, based on the artwork of "The Princess and the Pea" by
Tom Seidmann-Freud, 1921 (© Tom Seidmann-Freud Estate).

Original edition: © 2013 TASCHEN GmbH
Art Direction: Andy Disl and Noel Daniel, Los Angeles;
    Birgit Eichwede, Cologne
Editorial Coordination: Jascha Kempe, Cologne
Production Coordination: Thomas Grell, Cologne

Printed in Italy
ISBN 978-3-8365-4839-7